W0081792

# CURSED PRINCESS CLUB

## A MOST UNUSUAL PRINCESS

# CURSED PRINCESS CLUB

## A MOST UNUSUAL PRINCESS

# Michelle Knudsen

Based on the
Graphic Novel by

LambCat

wattpad books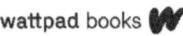

An imprint of Wattpad WEBTOON Book Group

Copyright © Wattpad WEBTOON Book Group, 2025

Based on the graphic novel by LambCat. © 2019 LambCat.

All rights reserved.

No portion of this publication may be reproduced or transmitted, in any form or by any means, without the express written permission of the copyright holders.

Published in Canada by Wattpad WEBTOON Book Group, a division of Wattpad WEBTOON Studios, Inc.

36 Wellington Street E., Suite 200, Toronto, ON M5E 1C7 Canada

*www.wattpad.com*

First Wattpad Books edition: November 2025

ISBN 978-1-99834-184-9 (Trade Paper original)
ISBN 978-1-83411-018-9 (eBook edition)

Names, characters, places, and incidents featured in this publication are either the product of the author's imagination or are used fictitiously. Any resemblance to actual persons (living or dead), events, institutions, or locales, without satiric intent, is coincidental.

Wattpad Books, Wattpad WEBTOON Book Group, and associated logos are trademarks and/or registered trademarks of Wattpad WEBTOON Studios, Inc. and/or its affiliates. Wattpad and associated logos are trademarks and/or registered trademarks of Wattpad Corp.

Library and Archives Canada Cataloguing in Publication information is available upon request.

Printed and bound in Canada

1 3 5 7 9 10 8 6 4 2

Cover design by Luz Tapia
Typesetting by Delaney Anderson

FOR PRINCESS TINA

# PROLOGUE

In the deep dark of the haunted forest, a door creaks slowly open.

Figures emerge, one after another. A swish of skirts, a clack of heels, a glint of jewelry.

A voice, dripping with anticipation: "I think we're going to have some fun tonight."

Murmurs of excitement as feminine shapes step into the moonlight. If anyone were watching, they would see the elegant dresses, the elaborately styled hair . . . and then they would see the rest. The *faces*. The zipper where a mouth should be. The impossibly long, pointed nose. The eyes that glow like tiny, malevolent suns.

The figures begin to descend the steps.

"Girls, wait," one says. "Do you hear that in the distance?"

The others listen. And then they hear it too—someone

running. Someone scared. Frantic footsteps through the undergrowth. Loud, panting breaths. Coming toward them.

"I believe a new friend has wandered into our forest." She smiles, a frightening flash of teeth in the dark. "Let's go say hello."

They vanish into the trees.

For several moments there is no sound at all.

And then the screaming begins.

# CHAPTER 1

## GWENDOLYN

Princess Gwendolyn of the Pastel Kingdom woke up with a smile on her face and a furry marsupial tangled in her hair.

"Mr. Possum, we've talked about this," she gently scolded as she reached up to pry him free. But it was no use; he was good and stuck. Again.

Gwen pushed back her blanket and bedsheets and sat up, startling Mr. Rat and sending him scurrying from where he'd been snuggled against her pillow. He looked at her reproachfully before settling down near the foot of the bed to start his morning grooming routine. Mr. Possum remained on her head like a very bitey night bonnet. He never sank his teeth all the way in, though. He was just using them to hang on, poor thing. He was a very anxious sleeper.

There was a knock at the door. "Gwendolyn? Are you awake?"

That was Papa's voice! He must have just returned from his latest journey. She'd thought he wasn't due back until later in the week. Gwen tried once more to tug Mr. Possum loose from her hair and then gave up and told her father to come in.

King Jack opened the door and leaned into the room, his pale purple crown resting neatly on his long gray hair. His clothes were still dusty from the road and he looked tired, but his face lit up with a delighted smile when he saw her. "I missed you, my cutie-pie!"

Gwen smiled back. He still treated her like she was five years old sometimes, especially when he'd been away for a while, but she didn't really mind so much. It was sweet how he doted on all four of his children. And as the youngest, she supposed it was only natural that he still thought of her as the baby, even though she was sixteen now. She knew that to everyone outside the family he was this fierce, inscrutable figure, but here at home, he was kind of a big teddy bear. Well, except when he was mad. Or when the topic of boys came up.

"I missed you, too, Papa! I'd give you a hug, but—" She gestured at Mr. Possum.

"Let me guess, that little critter is doing your hair?"

Mr. Possum growled, and Gwen laughed. Her father never seemed to remember that only Maria's animal friends were good at hair and makeup. "No, he's just . . . kinda stuck."

"Here, let me help." He strode over and tried to yank Mr. Possum free from Gwen's long, green tresses. Between his pulling and Gwen's cajoling and Mr. Rat nipping at his friend's tail, they finally succeeded. Mr. Possum slunk under the bed to regain his dignity.

The king straightened his crown, which had been knocked askew during the detangling. "Are you sure that creature is really the right kind of pet for a princess? I could ask Molly to have it removed—" He must have seen the horror on her face, because he held his hands up in surrender. "All right, all right. Your little friend stays."

"Both of them," Gwen said, scooping Mr. Rat into her arms protectively.

"Yes, yes, both of them. Whatever makes you happy, Gwennie. Speaking of which"—he grinned suddenly—"I have some really big news for you and your sisters. Please come downstairs as soon as you're ready."

"What kind of news?"

"Uh-uh," he said, backing away. "No spoilers! You'll have to come down and find out along with everyone else."

Gwen shook her head fondly. "All right, Papa." She waited for him to close the door and then got up and went to her wardrobe to change. She couldn't imagine what the really big news might be. He never shared much about his frequent expeditions, but perhaps this latest one had resulted in something wonderful for the kingdom? She knew how much it meant to him to be the best ruler he could possibly be.

Gwen picked out one of the dresses she'd made herself—a green and white one with orange bows going down the front—and brushed her hair, trying to get out the last of the possum-induced snarls at the ends. She pulled two strands to fall in front of her long, tapered ears and left the rest of her hair loose, which was her favorite way to style it. Her short, wavy bangs always did their own thing, so she'd learned not to fight with them. She thought they looked cute whatever they did anyway. Finally, she flashed herself a quick smile in the mirror—she'd read in one of Maria's magazines that smiling at yourself each morning was a good way to start your day off on a positive note. A few of her teeth were kind of pointy, which she thought made her smile look interesting as well as happy.

She stepped into her orange slippers (to match the bows on the dress) and at the last minute added a narrow pink ribbon belt, just because she liked it.

"Be good, boys," she told Mr. Possum—who had climbed back onto the bed once her father had gone—and Mr. Rat. She kissed each of them on their little noses and headed down to join her family.

~

All three girls reached the landing above the living room at the same time.

"Good morning!" Gwen gave each of her sisters a quick hug before they started down the stairs. Maria was the oldest at eighteen, with long, lustrous blond hair that the woodland creatures had styled today with two small braided buns at the top and pastel-blue ribbons to match the skirt of her blue and white dress. Lorena, next oldest at seventeen, wore a delicate headband with small pink blossoms (no doubt freshly picked from the gorgeous flowers that mysteriously burst into existence around her bed every night) that looked lovely against her shoulder-length, lavender hair. Gwen always felt she and her siblings looked like a beautiful pastel rainbow when they were all together. Especially when their brother Jamie was with them, all pink hair and sparkly eyes. Well, sparkly everything, really, since he always had a kind of ethereal glow about him. She liked to believe that their multicolored features (and various clothing preferences) reflected their personalities too: unique but complementary.

As the girls settled in on the couch, Papa sat down across from them and cleared his throat. "As you girls know, we are not the richest kingdom. There's no shame in that, but it's why I have to leave you so often to assist our men. I've made it hard on you, especially since your mother passed. And for that, I am deeply sorry."

Gwen exchanged concerned glances with her sisters. Papa

rarely spoke about their mother. And he had to know by now that they understood why he took these long journeys.

"We're fine, Papa!" Gwen assured him.

"Yeah," Lorena said. "You don't need to worry about us."

He smiled at that. "I know, you're all extremely capable. But, be that as it may, you're all growing up so quickly. And it's time we had a talk about your future and, um, the opposite sex."

Gwen groaned. "Oh, god, not 'the talk' again, Papa. Please don't lecture us for the hundredth time about how every man is a wolf with bad intentions."

"And then try to scare us by reading us 'The Three Little Pigs and the Big Bad Wolf' and telling us how they all want to blow our houses down," Maria added.

Lorena nodded in emphatic agreement. "Like we're gonna listen to you after you literally just called us pigs!"

"WELL, THEY *ARE* WOLVES!" the king shouted. Molly, the head maid, who had just entered with a tray of tea, made a very quiet, disapproving sound in the back of her throat, even though her expression remained composed as always. The king took a breath and lowered his voice. "I mean, no, I'm not talking about that today, girls. I know I've had some strict policies about allowing boys into your life . . ."

Lorena snorted, and Maria widened her eyes dramatically. Gwen bit her lip to keep from saying anything. The three girls had never in their whole lives been allowed to leave the palace grounds, let alone meet or talk to a boy besides their brother. The concept of actually going on a date or anything like that had always been entirely out of the question. The male guards in the castle weren't even allowed to look directly at their faces! The girls loved their father with all their hearts, but there was no denying that he was more than a little overprotective.

"Well, that changes today," the king continued. "For many years now, I've been in talks with my dear friend Leland, ruler of our longtime ally, the Plaid Kingdom. We've been discussing the idea of unifying our kingdoms and strengthening our bonds. Do you know what that means?"

"Yeah," Lorena muttered. "It means an impending fashion disaster because pastels and plaid look gross together."

"No," the king said. "Well, maybe. But also, it means I want to ask each of you to marry one of the princes from the Plaid Kingdom."

For a moment, the whole world seemed to stand still. The girls just stared at him, open-mouthed. Gwen was so shocked by what he'd said that her mind seemed to go completely blank. Marry? *Marry* one of the Plaid princes? She couldn't get the words to make sense in her head.

Lorena was the first to regain the power of speech. "Let me get this straight," she said. "You never let us even talk to boys, and now you're just asking us to marry strangers out of the blue?!"

Without really meaning to, Gwen asked, "And it's only because it will be beneficial for both kingdoms?" Her chest suddenly felt tight, like it was squeezing her heart. She hadn't ever really thought seriously about getting married—Maria had always been the romantic one—but now that Papa was talking about an arranged marriage, she suddenly realized how much she *did not like* that idea. If she ever got married, she wanted it to be to someone she loved! Or at least someone she knew and liked a whole lot. It was kind of hard to imagine what being in love would even feel like, since she'd never had the opportunity to experience it. But she definitely didn't want to spend the rest of her life with someone who just happened to be the right prince at the right time. What if he was a terrible person? And she had to live with him *forever*?

"Well . . ." Maria's voice shook Gwen out of her spiraling thoughts. "What do they look like?"

Gwen scoffed inwardly. That was hardly important! But as her father asked Molly to bring him the princes' portrait, she couldn't help being just a little bit curious.

Molly returned and handed a framed portrait to King Jack. He placed it on the table before them. Maria slowly reached forward and picked it up. Lorena leaned in to look, and after a second, Gwen did too.

*Oh*, was all she could think at first. *Oh my*.

The princes were absolutely gorgeous.

The image showed three young men who looked to be about the same ages as the princesses, or maybe just a little older. One, who must be the heir to the Plaid throne, sat in an ornate, golden chair in the center of the frame. He wore a red military-style shirt with a subtle plaid design and gray pants tucked into tall, dark boots. His auburn hair fell slightly in front of striking red eyes that glinted impishly at the viewer.

On the left, another prince posed on one knee, dressed similarly except that his plaid shirt was blue. His hair was a silver-blond color that perfectly complemented his strong-featured face, and he had a small scar on his right cheek that only seemed to enhance his rugged good looks. He winked out at them, one hand pressed against his heart.

But it was the third boy, the one kneeling on the right, who arrested Gwen's attention. He was obviously the youngest, like her, and his golden hair was unruly and seemed unable to decide which way it wanted to go. He was perhaps not quite as classically handsome as his brothers, but there was something about him that made her want to keep looking. A vulnerability, perhaps, that the older boys lacked. He was dressed in green, and his eyes were green too.

*My favorite color*, she found herself thinking.

Gwen wasn't sure how long they sat there staring at the picture, but eventually Maria handed it over to her and slowly stood up to face their father.

"This," she said to him, "is the happiest day of my life."

Lorena whooped and jumped onto the couch, ignoring

Molly's side-eye at shoes touching the furniture. "Best souvenir ever, Daddy!"

Gwen couldn't help being swept up in her sisters' happiness, all of her earlier concerns forgotten as she gazed into that third prince's charming, smiling face. She hugged the portrait to her chest and stared in amazement at her papa. "We're getting married to hunks!"

Papa didn't seem quite as excited as they were, but maybe he'd already gotten all his excitement out when he first made the arrangements. For some reason, Molly was patting him gently on the shoulder.

Finally, he raised his voice to be heard over his daughters' continued exclamations of joy. "Girls, calm down! There are still plenty of details to discuss!"

"Oh, that's right!" Maria said. She ushered the other girls back to their seats. "For instance, what are their names?"

"And their ages?" Lorena asked.

"Are they a big spoon or a little spoon?" Gwen put in. Her sisters turned to look at her, and she felt her face go red. "I—I read about that in a magazine," she said. "It seemed relevant?"

Papa studied the portrait. "Let's see. That's Lance on the left, he's nineteen; Blaine in the middle, he's twenty, and that's Frederick on the right, age seventeen. And . . . I suppose I can inquire about their silverware habits, though I don't why that matters."

"Since we're so close to the Plaid Kingdom," Gwen asked,

eager to move the conversation away from spoons, "how come we've never heard about these princes before?"

"Because they've been in military academies since they were tots and went straight into serving their country," the king explained. "I heard that the boys' perseverance was a real mental stronghold for their army."

"I'd like them to stronghold me in their armies," Maria whispered. Gwen choked on a laugh and Lorena snickered.

Papa pretended not to hear. "Their father is a man I know I can trust with my life, so I feel safe entrusting his sons with your happiness."

Gwen now felt a little silly for worrying that the princes might be awful in some way. Of *course* Papa wouldn't ask them to marry anyone he didn't think was a good match. And as princesses, they had a duty to do what was best for the kingdom. She tried to believe that was what she most cared about, and not the way that looking at that painting of Frederick made her feel.

"Do the princes know what we look like?" Lorena asked.

The king nodded. "Yes. I sent them a portrait of you as well, and they wrote back a note that said, 'Each daughter's beauty is nothing short of elysian.'"

"A lesion?" Lorena made a disgusted face. "Hmm. They're not very good at compliments. But whatevs, they're hot."

Gwen was about to clarify what *elysian* meant for Lorena—she knew her sister sometimes skipped their more poetic reading assignments to focus on martial arts and physical conditioning—but Maria spoke first. "So when do we get to meet them?"

"Ah." The king smiled brightly. "That's the best part of the surprise. They're coming for tea today! At two o'clock!"

Once again, the girls stared at their father in shock. Then, as one, they turned their eyes to the clock hanging on the wall. It was already eleven thirty.

Maria looked like she might throw up. Lorena and Gwen looked at each other in horror. "They're coming in two and a half hours?!"

The king seemed totally unaware of the effect his announcement had had on them. He took a breath and closed his eyes, gathering his thoughts in what they all knew was his I-am-about-to-make-you-listen-to-a-long-boring-lecture stance. "Now, my precious daughters, I want you to understand that your happiness and safety are a million times more important than our relationship with the Plaid Kingdom. But you may be wondering, what is happiness? Let me repeat a short tale from my past in which I encountered an omniscient clam, and it proclaimed that . . ."

Gwen didn't hear the rest because she was already tiptoeing up the stairs with her sisters.

"I can't wear this to meet my future husband!" Maria exclaimed when they reached the landing. "This is a *day princess* look for errands, like feeding swans or singing ballads from the balcony. I have to break out my evening gown!"

"Hey, could I get your birds to do my makeup?" Lorena asked her. "They're so much better at eyeliner than me."

"Definitely!" Maria said. "They do really know how to slay a cat eye."

Gwen hadn't even thought about makeup. She had a bigger problem. "My possum ate my evening gown," she said quietly.

Her sisters stopped at once and turned to her with reassuring smiles. "That's okay!" Lorena said. "I'll bring over some of my smaller evening gowns. Everything always looks lovely on you."

"Don't you worry," Maria said. "Your prince is totally going to fall for you no matter what you wear."

Gwen immediately felt relieved. Her sisters always looked out for her. And she tried to look out for them too. It was hard to worry about anything for long when she had her family to lean on. Sometimes they made her heart feel like it was simply going to explode with love. "Thanks, you guys," she said.

They all ran off to get ready. Just as Gwen approached Jamie's room, he opened the door and stepped out. Gwen blinked at the sudden sparkle in the air.

"Hey, Gwennie, what's going on? Where's everyone running off to?"

"Didn't Papa tell you? Oh, Jamie, it's the most exciting news! But also a little terrifying. Maybe a lot terrifying. But mostly really great? But—"

He laughed and took her by the shoulders, steadying her. "Take a breath, sis. What's this big news?"

"We're getting married!" she told him. "Me and Maria and Lorena! Well, engaged, anyway. Betrothed? I'm not sure what to call it. To the princes from the Plaid Kingdom! Papa says it's all arranged, but we still have to meet them and they're coming here today! For tea! In just over two hours!"

Jamie's eyes had gone wide. "Wow, that is big news! And you're—excited?" He looked at her carefully.

Gwen felt herself deflate, just a little. Jamie was her best friend, and he knew her better than anyone. "I want to be? I mean, I am. But it's all so sudden and sixteen does feel maybe a little young to be finding a husband?" A *husband*. The word felt so strange in her mouth.

"What do you know about the princes so far?"

"Not much," she admitted. "But we'll be getting to know them very soon, I guess! And we did get to see a portrait—" Frederick's face flashed before her eyes, and she felt herself blushing again.

Jamie, of course, noticed. He grinned at her. "I *see*," he said. "So that's how it is. Good-looking, is he?"

"Oh, Jamie," she said. "He's—they're—" She covered her face with her hands. "I'm being ridiculous, I know. You can't fall in love with a picture. And I'm not in *love*, obviously. But I just got this—this feeling . . ." She trailed off. If she'd been talking to anyone else, she would have been mortified right now. What was wrong with her?

Jamie gently pulled her hands away from her face. "It's okay to be excited," he said. "And not ridiculous at all to like the way he looks. But what really matters is how he treats you. And how you feel about him once you actually get to know him a little. You know that, right?"

"Yes," she said. "Yes, of course."

He smiled at her, reassuring her just like her sisters had done. Her heart inched even closer to bursting. "I'm sure he'll be delightful. Dad wouldn't ask you to marry anyone who wasn't."

She smiled back. "That's what I told myself too."

"Great minds think alike! Now go get ready. I suppose I should go talk to Dad and get the full scoop. I'm excited to meet the princes too! Also for tea! I'm starving!"

Gwen laughed and continued on her way to her room, walking now instead of running in a panic. Jamie always had such a calming effect on her. And his comment about being starving had given her a really great idea.

# CHAPTER 2

## GWENDOLYN

There was only one thing that could pretty much guarantee a successful afternoon tea.

Pie.

Fortunately, Gwen was very good at pie. She went to the compact but state-of-the-art kitchen connected to her rooms (her father had had it built for her before she was even tall enough to reach the counter without a step stool) and began preheating the oven while she gathered her ingredients. She'd make a few different flavors, since she didn't know what the princes would like best. Apple for one, definitely. And a peach cobbler. And maybe cherry? Blueberry? No—strawberry rhubarb, just to keep things interesting.

Baking was even more calming than talking to Jamie. Gwen felt herself relax into the familiar movements of combining the flour, salt, and sugar for the crusts in her prettiest mixing bowl. She had always loved making things, whether they were paintings, dresses, or desserts. But desserts were definitely her favorite. By the time she was cutting the chilled butter into the mixture, she felt almost herself again. She smiled thinking about both families sitting down together in a couple of hours, drinking tea and eating pie, all of them getting to know one another. Well, Papa already knew King Leland, of course—they'd been good friends forever. It did seem a bit odd that Papa had never once mentioned his friend's sons, but then, he kind of liked to pretend there was no such thing as boys (other than Jamie), so maybe it wasn't that odd after all.

She let herself envision a perfect afternoon as she worked on the fillings, everyone laughing and getting along wonderfully. She wondered which pie Frederick would choose. Maybe he would try them all. Maybe she would ask him what other kinds of pie he liked, and then she could make those next time. Maybe the Plaid Kingdom had some traditional desserts that she didn't even know about, and she could learn how to make those too. Maybe—this magical idea had just occurred to her—maybe Frederick liked to bake too! Maybe he could teach her his favorite recipes, and she could teach him hers. They could make up new ones together! She became momentarily quite absorbed by the vision of the two of them flitting around a kitchen in matching aprons, playfully flicking flour at each other's faces, tasting delicious things from each other's spoons.

Gwen hummed happily to herself as she brushed the tops of the pies with egg wash and sprinkled on a bit of sugar. She knew she shouldn't get too carried away. She didn't know anything about this boy besides what he looked like. She shouldn't make up ideas about his personality. But surely it couldn't hurt to daydream just a little.

She slid the pies into the oven. In forty minutes, the crusts would be golden brown and exactly the right amount of crispy. She was just starting to wonder how Maria's and Lorena's preparations were going when Lorena burst into the kitchen.

"There you are, Gwen! Come on, we have to plan!" She grabbed Gwen's arm and dragged her out without waiting for an answer.

Lorena pulled her gently but firmly down the hall to Maria's door, which she then flung open without knocking. "Tactical meeting!" Lorena said. "Now!"

Maria and Gwen got comfortable on Maria's bed while Lorena darted back into the hall. A few of Maria's bird and squirrel friends peered in from outside the window, waiting to see if Maria needed help getting ready. Soon Lorena returned, brushing stray flower petals from her shoulders and pulling a giant, wheeled chalkboard into the room behind her.

"All right," Lorena said. "We all know that we need to make

a great impression on the princes. Daddy has made it clear that this alliance is super important for our kingdom. And I think we can further agree that it is super important for us, personally, to end up romantically involved with those gorgeous examples of princehood. That is why I, as the military genius of the family, have devised a three-pronged offensive strategy that will ensure our conquest is successful."

She turned to the chalkboard and drew quick, surprisingly detailed stick-figure sketches while she explained her plan. "Phase one: the initial assault. When the princes arrive, we'll enter from the balcony with the advantage of high ground, and Maria will unleash long-range fire with some sexy stares." Gwen and Maria giggled as Lorena drew pictures of the princes being pelted by Maria's eyeball love arrows, with little word balloons coming from the boys saying things like *Too sexy!* and *My eyes!*

"Next," Lorena continued, "for phase two, I'll confuse them with some psychological warfare." Her next picture showed a bewildered Lance reacting to a stick-figure Lorena, saying *Hmph, you're not that cute. I can barely see your abs through your shirt.*

"Lorena," Gwen scolded. "We're not negging them into wanting our approval! I'm not okay with phase two."

"Fine, fine," Lorena said, waving her hands distractedly. "I'll come up with something else to knock down their guard. Then, for the final and all-important phase three, Gwen will enter into close-range combat through a blitz attack and tackle them into submission."

Her pictures this time showed Gwen flying through the air toward the princes, arms outstretched, and then the princes lying on the ground, little hearts floating around them.

"They won't know what hit 'em, but they'll be head over heels in love with us." Lorena grinned at her sisters. "Great plan, right?"

Gwen couldn't think of anything to say. She just kept staring at the chalk picture of her soaring through the air to tackle the princes.

Maria smiled at Lorena. "Um, I think it's a great start! However, it could benefit from one key addition." She reached over and pulled one of her many princess magazines from underneath her pillow. "According to all the latest fashion articles, attracting a prince may be only temporary, but a good bustle will make him stay forever!"

"A good what?" Lorena asked.

"A good bustle! You know, something that poofs up the back of your dress and makes you look, um, extra curvy!" She handed the magazine to Gwen and then knelt down to pull something from under the bed. The model in the illustrations wore a dress with piles of fabric that bunched up dramatically around her rear end. It . . . did not look natural. Gwen couldn't help scrunching up her nose. Princes *liked* that? She closed the magazine and put it down.

"Now, being the most fashion-forward sister," Maria went on, holding up a frightening-looking contraption made of pink-painted metal. "I already snuck out and bought the new Cinderella's Secret

Fairy God Bustle. It's an architectural marvel that provides three levels of increased lift. But you can pretty much stuff whatever you like up there. No need to overthink it." With that, she gave Lorena a lampshade and handed Gwen the royal pet cat, who had been curled up on Maria's light-blue duvet.

"Colonel Snuggles?" Gwen whispered, more than a little horrified at the idea of sticking their furry friend up under her skirt. Lorena looked equally uneasy about the lampshade.

"Come on!" Maria said, bending over and starting to hike up her dress. "Let's give them a try!"

"Wait!" Gwen said. She carefully placed Colonel Snuggles back on Maria's bed where he belonged. This was getting entirely out of hand. "Both of you, please. I appreciate all the effort you're putting into making sure the princes like us, but I think we're fine as we are! Without any special tactics or . . . butt architecture." She shuddered involuntarily. "I mean, if we're possibly going to spend the rest of our lives with these boys, doesn't it make more sense to just be ourselves? Don't we want them to get to know who we really are? Not some weird, violent, artificially big-bootied versions, but the real thing?"

Lorena looked thoughtful. "I suppose we do each have our own natural charms. Maria's the graceful one, I'm the strong one, Gwen's the crafty one—"

"And Jamie's the pretty one!" Maria put in, making them all laugh.

But as their laughter faded, Gwen suddenly had a new, terrifying thought. "Girls, if this works—I mean, if we all fall in love with the princes and get married—what happens then? Will we all have to move away? What if—what if we don't get to see each other anymore?"

Lorena and Maria both looked startled. "I hadn't thought about that," Lorena said. "Some tactician!"

"No," Maria said firmly, shaking her head. "That will never happen. It's true that these engagements would mean big changes to all of our lives, but no matter what, we'll always stay as close as we always have been." She sat on the bed and then scooted back, tucking her legs under her and making room for the others to sit too. Gwen and Lorena climbed onto the bed to join her. "Let's promise that, right now."

Maria held out her hands, and Gwen and Lorena each took one.

"I promise," Maria said, looking each of her sisters in the eye, "that nothing will ever come between us. Sisters forever."

"I promise too," Lorena said. "Sisters forever!"

"I promise too," Gwen echoed. "Sisters forever and ever and ever."

Lorena leaned forward and spread her arms wide. "Group hug!" Gwen, who just a second ago had been blinking back tears, found herself laughing again as she hugged her sisters back as hard as she could.

"All right, enough mushy stuff," Lorena said finally, extracting herself and bouncing onto her feet. "We're supposed to be getting ready! But I think Gwennie's right—no complex plans or complicated underwear. Let's just be our own fabulous selves."

"I guess I *could* forgo the bustle and wear a simple but elegant dress instead," Maria allowed.

"And maybe I'll just go for a quick run to calm my nerves instead of frantically creating assault schematics," Lorena said.

"And I'm baking some p—" Gwen started, then froze, staring at her sisters with wide eyes. "My pies!"

She'd completely forgotten about them. Without another word, she dashed from the room and back to her kitchen.

~

The pies were fine.

Gwen let out a big, relieved breath as she slid them out of the oven just in time. The crusts were a flawless golden brown, and the combined scent of the baked fillings was heavenly. She hated to slice into the unblemished circles of pastry, but it was necessary for the next step. There was just enough of a window left to ask Jamie to taste the pies before she served them to their guests. Normally she had total confidence in her baking but today was so important; she wanted to make sure everything was really perfect.

She cut a delicate sliver from each pie, arranged them on a

plate, and set them on a tray with a fancy dessert fork and a folded linen napkin. Then she poured a tall glass of sparkling apple cider to accompany the little tasting array. She was pretty lucky that the kingdom's most respected food critic lived just down the hall! Jamie was renowned not only for his expertise in all cuisines but also—and especially—for his frighteningly discerning tongue. He could taste the smallest hints of flavor in any dish, which was perhaps to be expected from any serious food critic. But he could *also* taste what the cook had been feeling while preparing the food. This lent an extra depth to his evaluations, and chefs from even the farthest countries would sometimes visit to consult with Jamie on their craft.

It was a beautiful day, so she'd sent a servant ahead to ask Jamie to meet her on the little garden patio. It was one of the loveliest spots outside the palace, with a couple of ivory-colored tables and chairs set out on smooth white paving stones surrounded by a neatly trimmed emerald-green lawn. Benches beckoned invitingly at regular intervals along the enclosing wrought-iron fence while pretty little birds fluttered between elegant stone birdbaths. Luscious rose bushes lined the other side of the fence, and, through some kind of landscaping magic, the flowers were always in full bloom. Jamie was already sitting outside, pink hair glinting in the sunlight, when she arrived.

"Thanks for making time for me, Jamie!"

"No prob, sis." He eyed the pies appraisingly. "Don't give me too much credit, though. It's not like tasting your baking is exactly a hardship. I always love everything you make, Gwennie."

"Aw, you're so sweet," she said. "I guess I'm just a little nervous today. I really want to make a good impression!"

"Well, if these pies taste half as good as they look, I'm sure the princes will love them." He patted the tablecloth in front of him. "Let's find out. Serve me up!"

Suddenly another voice, harsh and deep, rang through the peaceful afternoon quiet. "Intruder on the premises! All guards on red alert!"

Gwen nearly dropped the plate. "Oh no!" She turned, and over the tops of the rose bushes, she could just make out the sight of guards rushing past, weapons at the ready. "Papa *has* mentioned that there's been an increase in crime and petty sorcery lately. But I didn't think he meant here at the palace!" She started to turn back. "Jamie, we'd better get insi—"

She froze in shock. There was a stranger on the patio, standing inches from her brother.

Jamie appeared equally shocked. He was staring, mesmerized, at the intruder, not even pulling back as the woman reached out to caress his chin with one long, bony finger. She wore a sweeping, black hooded robe, and her scraggly white hair hung limply around her gray face.

*A witch*, Gwen realized, panic making her heart stutter. Not every witch was evil, but a good witch probably wouldn't have felt the need to sneak in past the castle defenses. And bad witches could be *really* bad news, especially if you made them angry. Did Jamie know that? He still hadn't moved.

The witch was completely fixated on Jamie. "Why, hello," she crooned at him. "What a pretty princess you are." Without breaking eye contact, she produced a bright-red apple half-coated in sticky pink glaze. A jaunty red-and-white striped stick extended from its center. "Won't you have a bite of this delicious candied apple?"

"Um, excuse me," Gwen said, finally able to make herself speak. "May I ask what you're doing?"

The witch's head snapped up, and she stared at Gwen in confused alarm. She must not have noticed anyone else was there. Then her eyes widened in seeming recognition.

"Oh! Hey, my bad, sister! I didn't see you!" She raised one hand before her, palm out, in a placating gesture. "You were clearly here first. I did not mean to encroach on your prey. No hard feelings, right?"

Gwen blinked at her. "I—"

"Us ladies got to look out for each other, you know!" The witch made a little clicking sound with the side of her mouth and pointed at Gwen. "Solidarity, am I right?" She glanced at the apple in her hand and then set it down on the table. "Hey, here's a peace offering. I'll just leave it here in case you need a little backup." Then she dropped to the ground and crawled through a hole in the fence, disappearing into the rose bushes. "Toodles!" she called as she vanished.

For a moment Gwen just stared after her. "What the heck was that about?" She shook her head. "Well, anyway, let's—"

She broke off in appalled horror as she once again turned back to her brother, who was taking a big bite of candied apple.

"Jamie, noooo!!!!" she screamed. But she already knew it was too late.

Jamie's eyes went wide and glassy. "I taste nutmeg, vanilla . . . and sleeping potion."

Then he fell face-first onto the table, out cold.

# CHAPTER 3

## FREDERICK

As the royal Plaid carriage pulled to a stop, Frederick fought to keep his expression relaxed. If his brothers realized he was nervous, he would never hear the end of it. Blaine and Lance didn't *get* nervous. They just always assumed everything would work out great, because it always did. For them. They breezed through life with their perfect faces and perfect skills and perfect everything else, and the world just showered them with success at every turn. Sadly, whatever magical blessings the universe had given his older siblings seemed to have run out by the time Frederick was born.

*Stop it*, he told himself. There was no sense sitting here feeling resentful. It wasn't like his brothers could *help* being perfect. And he didn't want to ruin his mood thinking about them. This was a special day. Maybe the day his whole life would change. Maybe the universe had just been saving up its blessings for him, to deliver all at once, right now.

He stepped onto the cream-colored pavement and stood beside Blaine and Lance at the Pastel Palace's front entrance. The place certainly lived up to its name. Pale, iridescent stone walls stretched up into towers topped with scallop-edged, conical roofs in shades of cotton candy and amethyst. Even the surrounding landscape seemed to be actively participating in the color scheme. Fluffy white clouds drifted through a powder-blue sky, and bright green grass spread invitingly across the grounds, dotted with oversized, pink-hued flowers. It was all very pretty, Frederick supposed, although he preferred their own stately and dignified Plaid Palace back home. But he suspected he would learn to love this palace, given who he now knew lived inside. He stretched his arms behind him, trying to work out the kink in his lower back from the bumpy journey.

Lance nudged him with one elbow, hard, knocking him off balance. "Ready to meet your dream girl, li'l bro?"

"Shut up, Lance," Frederick said, but he was careful not to put any real emotion in his voice. Totally nonchalant, that was the vibe he was going for. Meeting their future wives? Cool, cool. Finally connecting in person with the most beautiful girl he had ever seen? No big deal at all. He wished he had even a fraction of his brothers' confidence, but he didn't. So he'd fake it, and no one would ever know the difference.

He just wished he could fool himself too. *She's never going to like you*, the mean little voice in his head was already insisting. *She's going to be so disappointed that you're the one she's stuck with.*

*Shut up*, he told the voice. If she was half the girl he imagined her to be, she would see right past the faults that other people always found in him. She wouldn't be concerned with superficial things like whether he was as popular as Blaine or as strong as Lance. She'd see that he had value to offer too.

"All right," Blaine said, clapping his hands together twice. "Let's go meet the ladies!"

With one last steadying breath, Frederick followed his brothers up the walkway to the palace.

An older woman with a serene, kindly face met them at the door. She was a servant of some kind, her uniform neat and tasteful and entirely in shades of buttercream yellow. She bowed to the exact degree appropriate to their positions as princes of a neighboring kingdom, then straightened with a smile. "Welcome, Your Highnesses. We are so honored by your visit. Won't you please come this way?"

As she led them down the long hallway, Frederick stole glances at the pastel surroundings. It was hard to focus on anything but his growing excitement, however. It seemed to take forever to reach the doorway at the end of the corridor.

The woman paused, holding a hand up to bid them wait, and then said in a carrying voice, "Pardon the intrusion, Your Majesty, but the princes of the Plaid Kingdom have arrived." Then she stepped aside and gestured the boys into the room before them.

Frederick caught barely more than a glimpse of King Jack and the girls walking alongside him before Lance jabbed him with another elbow as he dropped to one knee. Frederick quickly followed suit, furious with himself for almost messing up already. They had gone over the protocol a hundred times! He had to pull it together. He had to make a perfect first impression.

"Your Majesty," Blaine said formally. "We are deeply honored to have been invited to your kingdom. Father was very eager to visit but got held back by some important affairs, so he had us make the trip alone."

Frederick had been thrilled when Father announced he wasn't coming with them. He was nervous enough on his own, and Father made him feel even more awkward and incompetent than his brothers did. None of them needed the extra pressure of having King Leland breathing down their necks during this first, incredibly important meeting.

"Oh, that's quite all right," King Jack said jovially as the boys got to their feet. The king's voice was deep and commanding, but he seemed a lot friendlier than Frederick would have expected a good friend of his father's to be. Father was so strict and angry all the time. King Jack, standing there in his lavender robes and crown and wearing a big smile seemed, well, nice. "Tell your pops I'll just kick his flannelled butt at chess some other day!" Blaine smiled uncertainly, and Frederick nearly winced. There was no way any of them were going to say that to Father.

"But enough about us old geezers," King Jack went on. "Let's have you kids introduce yourselves!" He placed a hand behind each of the girls standing beside him and shoved them firmly forward. "Go on now, girls!" At the princesses' stricken expressions, he shook his head fondly. "Sorry, gents. I may have raised them to be a little shy around boys."

But Frederick was hardly concerned with any of that. By now he had managed to count the number of girls, which was two, and also to confirm that, while they were both very beautiful, neither of them was the vision of ultimate enchantment that he had seen in the portrait. He stared around the room, as though she might be tucked out of sight behind the curtains or something. Where was she?

The blond princess quickly recovered some of her poise. She curtsied daintily, holding the edges of her light-blue dress with delicate fingers. Then she blinked sea-green eyes at them and stammered, "M-m-my name is Maria! We've heard so much about the Plaid Kingdom. It-it-it's a pleasure to minally feet you!" Her face turned the color of ripe tomatoes as she realized what she'd just said.

Blaine, perfect as always, stepped forward and grasped her hands, smiling reassuringly. "My name is Blaine, and the pleasure is all mine to be able to stand in the presence of someone so radiant."

The girl seemed in danger of losing her own ability to stand as she gazed at Blaine, apparently overwhelmed by both his irritatingly incredible good looks and his kindness in completely ignoring her verbal slipup.

Then the other princess spoke up, slightly more confidently than the first. Her peach dress draped fashionably on a somewhat sportier figure than her sister, which suggested at least one thing in common with Lance. Of *course* Lance would magically manage to find a fiancé who might actually be interested in the details of his workout routines and physical accomplishments. They'd probably be arm wrestling happily before the afternoon was over. "Uhhh, hi. My name is Lorena. I'm super stoked to meet you all."

Lance didn't miss a beat. Just like Blaine, he stepped toward the girl and took her hands in his. "I'm Lance, and I think you're more beautiful than a million red roses."

Frederick rolled his eyes before he could help himself, but it didn't matter, because no one was looking at him. Blaine and Lance and the princesses were all staring goofily into one another's eyes, and the king was staring goofily at all four of them. Frederick could practically see little hearts floating in the air around them. Which was all very nice and stuff, but . . .

"Uh, hi, everyone," he heard himself saying. "My name is Frederick, and I thought there was a third daughter . . . ?"

Lance tore his gaze away from his lavender-haired princess to shoot Frederick a smug sideways glance. "Ya snooze, ya lose, li'l bro."

"Shove it, Lance!" Frederick snapped, unable this time to pretend he didn't care. Not about the two princesses in the room—about the missing one. That third princess was the only one he wanted. He thought she might be *everything* he wanted. He knew how foolish that sounded, especially since he had only ever seen her picture. But somehow, deep inside, he felt it was true. These girls were very attractive, sure, but the other one had already stolen his heart.

"Uh, yes," said King Jack, also pulling his gaze away from the lovefest. "She's running behind but will be here as quickly as—"

"Sorry I'm late!" a female voice called as another door to the parlor swung open.

"Well, speak of the devil!" the king said. "There she is!"

A servant burst in, carrying the princess in her arms. Some part of Frederick realized this was odd—was the princess *sleeping?*—but it was hard to think clearly past the sudden, overwhelming joy that suffused his entire being. He'd been starting to fear that he'd dreamed her up somehow, imagined the perfect angel he'd seen in the portrait, but no, there she was. She was real. The girl he was going to marry. The girl who would change everything.

"Whoa," Blaine and Lance said in unison.

"There she is," Frederick said aloud. "The most beautiful woman I've ever seen in my life."

The servant—a strange-looking girl with yellow-green skin and seaweed-colored hair—stumbled to a stop, and the princess slumped to the floor, head and shoulders cradled in the strange young woman's arms. It began to finally register that something was wrong. What was going on? Was she ill? Injured? He wanted to run to her, but the king got there first.

"What on earth happened?!" King Jack said, staring down in alarm.

"Poisoned apple from a witch," the servant said. "I couldn't stop it in time."

The servant looked like she could be the witch herself—she had that unattractive witchy appearance, and were some of her teeth kind of . . . pointed?—but she was apparently known to the family, so she must just happen to be unfortunate in her lineage.

The king seemed more frustrated than upset by the girl's news. He closed his eyes briefly and pressed the bridge of his nose with two fingers. "I swear, that child gets in more trouble than a cat wearing boots." Then he turned to the yellow-uniformed woman. "Molly, can you please take care of the necessary arrangements?"

"Right away, Your Majesty." She helped the witchy-looking girl to lift the princess again and together they carried her out the door. Frederick stared after them, concern twisting his heart. Should he offer to go with them? To help? He didn't know her yet, it probably wouldn't be appropriate, but—

King Jack shook his head, then turned back to the princes, smiling once again. "Well, anyhow, now that all the daughters are here, let's get on with the marriage talks, shall we?"

What? The girl needed medical attention! Blaine and Lance were obviously as shocked as he was.

"But she looked unconscious!" Blaine objected. "Surely we can postpone things until your daughter has recovered!"

King Jack blinked at him. "What are you talking about? That was my son, Jamie. My daughter Gwendolyn was the one carrying him."

"That was your son?!" Blaine asked, unable to keep the consternation from his voice.

"That was your daughter?!" Frederick asked, unable to keep the horror from his.

The world went sort of gray and fuzzy around the edges. Frederick tried to process what the king had just said. It couldn't—it couldn't be true. He had mistaken the *son* for the youngest daughter? The *son* was that beautiful pink-haired angel? And that witchy girl—he couldn't—there had been a frightening-looking figure in one corner of the portrait with the princesses, but he'd barely looked at it, assuming it was just an evil spirit haunting the picture. It happened all the time with portraits at their palace. But apparently it hadn't been an evil spirit. That *thing* had been his intended bride! *So . . . I was attracted to . . . and I'm about to be engaged to . . .* He couldn't finish either thought.

Dimly, he felt Lance's strong arm guiding him to a sofa. He sat down, blinking hard, trying to regain control of himself. He was not going to embarrass himself or his brothers. He was a Plaid prince, and he was going to act like one. He'd pretend everything was fine until he could make some excuse to get them out of there. This had all been a terrible mistake. They'd get back home and explain everything to Father, and his engagement would be called off. There was no way his father would force him to marry—that.

As if on cue, the third daughter reappeared in the doorway, carrying a tray. She was smiling now, which did nothing to improve her appearance. Those teeth were definitely pointed. She practically had fangs! She was wearing a hideous green and white dress with ridiculous orange bows all down the front. There was no way anyone could blame Frederick for his confusion. Nothing about her looked remotely princess-like at all.

"Please excuse my tardiness! My name is Gwendolyn, and I'm incredibly happy to make your acquaintance. Also, I baked some pies!" She stepped closer, and Frederick saw that the tray held a neat arrangement of plates with little triangles of different crusts and fillings.

Blaine and Lance seemed to have recovered completely. "Wow! Thank you, Gwendolyn," Blaine said politely, taking an offered plate. "I'm Blaine, by the way."

Lance was already snatching a plate from the tray before the girl could even finish turning toward him. "I'm Lance, and this looks delicious!"

*You can do this*, Frederick told himself. *Just act like your brothers.*

"Uh, hey, Gwendolyn. I'm Frederick. Nice to meet you." He

was staring, he could feel it. He had to say something else. "So, uh, tell me, what happened to your sis—er, brother again?"

"Oh, he ate a poisoned apple from a witch," she said, her smile widening as she handed him a piece of pie with a slender slice of apple on top. "Enjoy!"

Frederick took the plate, trying to stop his hands from shaking. "Th—thank you."

He stared down at his pie, unable to say anything else, unable to do anything else, unable to make himself take a bite. Beside him, he heard Lance chomping enthusiastically away. Blaine had probably started eating his pie too. He wanted to make them stop. He wanted to yank the plates away and smash them on the floor. What if she was trying to poison them all?

No, that couldn't be right. She wasn't really a witch. She just looked like one. He had to calm down. They weren't really in any danger. The only thing that would die here tonight was his dream. He should have known by now that nothing would ever go right for him. The universe hadn't been holding some secret blessings in reserve to surprise him with. Somehow, this werewolf of a day had transformed in an instant from wonderful to monstrous. A nightmare.

He sat and clutched his plate and tried not to feel anything at all as the last slivers of his heart's hope crumbled into dust.

# CHAPTER 4

## GWENDOLYN

Once everyone had been served, Gwen placed the tray with the remaining portions of pie on the sideboard. She stood there for a few minutes, her back to the room, fussing with the plates and trying to catch her breath. The encounter with the witch and Jamie's confounding decision to bite the apple had been a very effective distraction from her nervousness, but it also meant she hadn't had any time to change or fix her hair or anything. She knew she'd been the one telling her sisters they should just be themselves, but she'd intended to be herself in one of Lorena's lovely gowns! She liked what she was wearing well enough, but it probably wasn't exactly appropriate for a first meeting with her potential fiancé.

She snuck a glance at Frederick out of the corner of her eye.

He was just as attractive in person as he'd been in the portrait. All of the princes were. The older boys were already chatting with Papa, Maria, and Lorena, but Frederick was quiet, looking down at his pie. Maybe he was as nervous as she was?

Lorena murmured something about needing a fork and then came up to stand beside Gwen. "You okay?" she asked softly.

"Oh, yes," Gwen said. "I was just about to sit down and join you all."

After a quick look back at the others, Lorena leaned over and whispered into Gwen's ear. "I don't want to jinx it, but I think things are going really well!"

Lorena's eagerness made Gwen smile. She knew she'd been late to the party, but she hadn't been *that* late. Her sisters could barely have exchanged more than a handful of words with the princes. She was glad to know Lorena didn't think Jamie's untimely unconsciousness had ruined the afternoon, though.

Gwen and Lorena joined Maria on the sofa across the low coffee table from the second sofa, where the boys were sitting. Papa was in his favorite chair at one end of the table, one-third of the way through his serving already.

"Gwennie, this is fantastic!" he said, beaming at her.

Blaine and Lance made enthusiastic sounds of agreement around their mouthfuls of pie. She'd given Blaine the strawberry rhubarb, and Lance had grabbed the peach cobbler.

"Thank you!" she said, smiling at them. She glanced again at

Frederick, who hadn't said anything. In fact, he hadn't even taken a bite yet. She'd given him the apple without thinking; maybe he would have preferred a different flavor?

One of the kitchen staff came in with tea for everyone, and for a moment they were all distracted by choosing between the offerings—Chef Martina had brewed three of the fanciest blends today—and adding milk or honey or sugar (or in Lance's case, all three).

"So," Maria began, once they'd all settled back in their seats, "let's get to know each other! What do you all like to read? Do you enjoy fairy tales?"

"Oh, I don't read fairy tales," Blaine said. "They're a bit too sappy and childish for my taste."

Lance snorted. "Right. Like your books about dragons and secret treasures are so realistic."

"Fairy tales are *not* childish!" Lorena said indignantly. She pointed her fork at Blaine. "Did you ever read the Crimm Brothers' version of 'Cinderella'? That's the real stuff right there. The wicked stepsisters can't fit into the glass slipper, so they grab a knife and cut off their—"

"Ew!" Gwen interjected. "Lorena!"

"But then," Lorena went on, "it gets better! Because later these pigeons show up and peck out their—"

"Stop!" Maria ordered, glaring at Lorena. "Do not make me vomit in front of company today!"

Lorena lowered her fork, which she'd been using to demonstrate the pigeons' pecking. "Sorry, Maria." But then she winked at Gwen, totally undermining the apology.

Gwen laughed before she could stop herself. Lorena was always a little more violent than Maria would like. Maria couldn't stay mad, though, and after a second, she laughed too.

"You'll have to excuse my sister," she told the boys. "She has unusual tastes when it comes to books."

"I think it's cool," Lance said. "I've read that story too. The pigeon part is the best!"

"Pigeons are not nearly as exciting as dragons," Blaine muttered. Then he seemed to realize he might be insulting Lorena as well as his brother. "I mean, I'm sure those particular pigeons are, um . . ." He trailed off, then shook his head, smiling ruefully. "Sorry, I've got nothing. I'm afraid I'll take dragons over pigeons any day."

"Team dragon!" Maria said, raising a fist in the air and laughing.

Gwen glanced at Frederick again, who was the only one not joining in. *He must be really shy*, she thought. She hadn't gotten to talk to him much at all. They hadn't said anything to each other since she'd given him his slice of pie. Which he still hadn't tasted.

She was trying to think of something she could ask him to draw him out—she was afraid asking him anything about cooking would make it seem like she was hinting about his uneaten pie—when her father abruptly cleared his throat.

"Well, it seems like everyone is hitting it off swimmingly!" he said. "We knew you'd all like one another. What's not to like? Three fine boys, three lovely girls. And excellent parentage all around. So! Shall we move along with the marriage arrangements? Maybe have some royal dates and movie nights?" He stopped and narrowed his eyes suddenly. "Chaperoned, of course."

"Absolutely," Blaine said at once.

"I'd love th—" Lance began.

"Uh, actually," Frederick broke in, finally speaking up, "I just remembered—we promised we'd check in with Father before we agree to anything. So, um, we should really be heading out about now."

His brothers looked astonished. "Frederick, what are you—"

"Blaine, don't you remember? Father said it, uh, right as we were leaving. Since he couldn't come along with us. Remember?" He was staring at Blaine very hard.

"Oh, of course," Maria said politely. "We've kept you for too long."

"No, you haven't," Lance said. "I don't know what Frederick is talking about. I'm not going anywhere. There's still some pie left and it's stupid good." He stood up and walked to the sideboard, then grabbed the rest of the peach cobbler and held it up. "Anyone mind if I finish this?"

"Lance, no!" Frederick shouted. He ran over to try to pull the pie from his brother's hands, but he was clearly no match for the bigger boy, who simply held him at arm's length with one strong hand. "Ow! Stop it!" Frederick said, struggling in vain to get closer. His face was turning red with effort and emotion. "Stop grabbing another slice!"

Gwen looked at her sisters, who seemed just as confused as she was. Even if the princes were supposed to consult with King Leland before making any plans, it shouldn't mean they had to leave so soon. The conversation had just gotten started. Was this her fault somehow? Maybe Frederick had been insulted by her lateness. Or maybe he'd been offended by Lorena's eye-pecking-pigeon reenactment? Or maybe he hated pie?

No, that wasn't possible. No one hated pie.

Blaine stood up a bit stiffly. "I suppose we really do need to depart now," he said, sounding regretful. He shot Frederick an unreadable glance, then turned back to the rest of them. "Thank you, King Jack. And princesses, I don't know when we shall meet again, but I hope—"

"One moment, Blaine," Papa said. He gestured to Molly, who had just appeared in the doorway. "Yes, Molly? Is everything—"

"Please pardon the interruption, Your Majesty. Arrangements for Prince Jamie's wake tonight have been taken care of, but I need your approval for the invitations before we send them out." She handed him a piece of parchment.

"A wake?!" Blaine blurted, his formal demeanor vanishing. "My god! Your son died?!"

"That's—that's awful," Lance whispered. Frederick seemed speechless with dismay beside him.

"What? No!" Papa said. He waved his hands in a calm-down gesture. "No, no—a *wake*. You know, short for wake-up ceremony. Because the witch made him magically fall asleep."

The boys just stared blankly at him. Gwen thought they really needed to read more fairy tales.

The king continued to explain. "It's a social event in our kingdom where people from all over gather to try to wake the sleeping beauty—er, person."

"Oh," Blaine said, visibly relieved but still also visibly trying to regain his composure. "Oh, okay. Yeah, that's not how that term is used, generally."

"You'll stay for it, right?" Maria said, abandoning her earlier effort to let them off the hook and latching onto this excuse to keep them around longer. "It's customary to attend a wake of someone you've met!"

"And you did *technically* meet Jamie," Lorena said, "even though he was asleep."

"And he was poisoned while he was helping me with the pies," Gwen put in, trying to do her part. "So in a way, we're all a little responsible!" She blinked up at the princes with her best puppy-dog eyes, knowing her sisters were doing the same. "Please?"

"Pretty please?" Maria and Lorena added.

Blaine and Lance turned their own puppy-dog eyes to Frederick. "Yeah, pretty please?"

Based on his contorted expression, Frederick seemed to be

having some kind of fierce internal battle. Maybe trying to weigh his father's original instructions against the social demands of the new circumstances, which of course his father could not have predicted. Gwen sympathized; it could definitely be hard to know what to do in complicated situations like this. Especially when everyone was staring at you. Finally, he sighed. "Yes. Yes, of course we should attend. It's the only right thing to do."

Maria gave a quiet little squeal and Lorena whisper-shouted, "Yes!"

*Thank you, Jamie,* Gwen whispered inside her head. She'd been quite upset with him for biting the apple—he should have known better than to accept sweets from a strange witch!—and of course she had been worried, too, but she forgave him everything now. Besides, surely someone would be able to wake him up again. There was always *some* way to break a spell, wasn't there?

Everyone seemed thrilled at the princes' decision to stay . . . except Frederick. It was hard to read his face, but he definitely didn't look happy. He sank back down onto the sofa and started poking little holes in his pie with his fork. Then bigger holes. He still hadn't eaten any of it.

Gwen was tempted to offer him some of the strawberry rhubarb instead, in case he just really hated apple and hadn't wanted to be rude. (Lance had polished off the rest of the peach cobbler, so that was no longer an option.) But her feet felt glued to the floor. If she offered and he said yes, she could bring him another plate and then sit down next to him. She could ask him what other flavors he liked, and didn't like, and maybe even promise to make him something special for next time.

But what if he said no to the strawberry rhubarb? Then what would she do? She could still try to sit down next to him, but the pie-flavor conversation might not work then. It might sound accusatory, like, *If you don't like apple or strawberry rhubarb, do you even like anything? Are you some kind of monster?* She could try to go back to the reading topic, but he hadn't participated at all the first time, so maybe he didn't like books either. *Or,* she tried to tell herself, maybe he was just too shy to speak in the larger group. Maybe he would welcome a quiet conversation with just one person. Maybe he would look up at her gratefully when she approached, and stop stabbing his poor uneaten glob of fruit and crust, and ask her to sit down and talk, just the two of them.

But she still couldn't make herself walk over to him.

"Please excuse me for a moment," Gwen said to no one in particular. Then she turned and headed for the balcony. A little fresh air was what she needed.

The late afternoon sun was bright in the sky, and she turned to it like a flower, closing her eyes and soaking in its warmth. She concentrated on breathing slowly in and out, trying to release the tension she felt in her body. She wasn't used to feeling so uncomfortable. Perhaps it was only to be expected; given Papa's overprotective tendencies, she spent most of her time with family and the castle staff, all of whom had known her since she was a baby. She didn't have much experience being around strangers. And really, this day had been somewhat of an emotional whirlwind! Papa returned from his journey, the girls found out they were going to be engaged, Jamie got poisoned by a witch . . . all within just a few hours. No wonder she felt out of sorts.

She opened her eyes and turned around, leaning against the balcony railing. Through the open door she saw her sisters and Blaine and Lance talking animatedly, her father looking on with obvious satisfaction. No one seemed to notice she was gone. No one was paying any attention to Frederick either. He was still on the sofa, torturing his pie, his handsome face despondent. Maybe he felt as awkward as she did. His brothers both had rather big personalities from what she'd seen so far; it couldn't be easy being the youngest if he was on the shy side. He had also been the only one trying to follow their father's directive, and although Blaine came around eventually, Lance had simply dismissed Frederick's earnest reminder. Maybe she needed to be a little more patient. It wasn't fair for any of them to expect the princes to just fall instantly in love with them.

Her gaze slid back to the other couples. True, the rest of them did seem to be hitting it off pretty quickly. But there was nothing wrong with taking things slowly. Some things just took time. Like baking a pie. If you tried to rush it, you just got bad pie. She wanted to have good pie with Frederick. Really good pie. She had to let things take whatever time they needed.

Voices on the grounds below caught her attention, and she turned around again. A faction of castle guards had apparently been tasked with delivering the invitations to Jamie's wake. The one in charge seemed to be giving the rest instructions; he was pointing and gesturing with one hand while holding up a pink envelope in the other.

Suddenly a small black crow darted down, snatched the envelope from his hand, and flew away. The guard yelped and Gwen covered her mouth, surprised by her own laughter. The poor man looked so bewildered, staring after the thieving bird as his fellow guards guffawed and clapped him consolingly on the back. Gwen was sure Molly, who always thought of everything, had arranged for extra invitations just in case—although she probably hadn't foreseen "stolen by crow" as one of the possible mishaps!—so the guard wouldn't get in trouble or anything. So it was probably okay for Gwen to be laughing along with the others.

And she had really needed the laugh! Her tension had finally drained away, and she felt ready to go back inside. She would think of Frederick as a special pie that just needed a little extra time in the oven. And thanks to Jamie, now she had the rest of the evening to try to talk to him. Perhaps the larger social event would paradoxically give her more of a chance to speak with him alone.

She could invite him to step away from the crowds with her to find someplace quiet.

Armed with her revised perspective and tentative plans, Gwen shook off the remnants of her pensive mood and headed back inside.

# CHAPTER 5

## GWENDOLYN

The princes were led off to a private suite to rest up and refresh themselves before the evening's festivities, while the girls helped Molly with the arrangements. Molly had a full staff to help her, of course, but setting up for the wake was too much fun to miss. Gwen volunteered to help with the buffet menu while Lorena supervised the erection of the game booths and Maria organized the petting zoo. (None of them wanted to help with the clowns.)

Gwen loved the energy of everyone running around, trying to get things ready. She and her sisters had been allowed to help with party setups before, but in the past they'd never actually been allowed to stick around for the party itself. This time, since the princes would be there, expecting the princesses' company, Papa couldn't justify sending the girls up to their rooms. Knowing they would get to stay this time made all of the prep work seem extra exciting.

The hours flew by—they only had about three of them, since the wake was scheduled to begin at six o'clock—but under Molly's leadership, the palace looked perfect by then. The clocks chimed the hour just as the first carriages began pulling up and unloading their various passengers. Everyone was dressed in their best semiformal wake wear, and they were clearly delighted at this unexpected opportunity to gather at the castle and mingle with the royal family. And for the chance, for whoever wanted to try, to be the one to wake up Jamie.

Unfortunately, before the princesses could escape to enjoy themselves, Papa insisted they stand with him at the entrance to the ballroom to greet the guests. He arranged them on either side of the archway just past the BALLROOM C signage. As each person or group entered, they all had to smile and welcome them and respond politely to whatever random things the guests said.

"Ughhh, I can't believe this," Lorena said in between smiling and welcoming people. "We convinced the princes to stay for Jamie's wake, but now we're not allowed to go spend time with them!"

Papa frowned and made one of his this-is-for-your-own-good faces. "Now, girls, if I'm going to allow you to attend these mixed-company events, then at the very least you must first carry out your royal responsibility of greeting our gracious guests."

Normally Gwen would have been thrilled to be meeting all of these people for the first time, but tonight all she wanted to do was find Frederick. Although, as they stood there saying hello to guest after guest who wanted to comment on how lovely they were and how nice it was to finally meet them and how—*ha-ha*—they'd all started to think the king had just made up having daughters, she started feeling anxious again. On the balcony earlier, she'd managed to convince herself that everything was fine. But the more she replayed the afternoon's events in her mind, the less sure she became. Blaine and Lance had seemed so happy to meet her sisters, so eager to get to know them. Frederick had seemed like he just wanted to leave from the moment she'd arrived.

Maybe . . . maybe Frederick wasn't the problem. Maybe the problem was her. Maybe he'd somehow already decided that he didn't want to marry her. Although she didn't know how he could make that call after barely even *talking* to her.

After the five hundredth time that Maria and Lorena begged their father to let them go—Maria's smiles at the people entering were starting to look strained, and Lorena's were positively feral— he finally relented.

"All right, all right," he said, shaking his head in surrender. "I suppose it is only proper for you to escort the princes around the party. They are our special guests, after all, and they probably won't know anyone else here."

Lorena dashed away before the words were even out of Papa's

mouth. Maria grabbed Gwen's wrist and started after her. But Gwen's feet were feeling heavy again.

Maria noticed at once. "Gwennie, is anything wrong?"

Gwen opened her mouth to say no, of course not, but she couldn't quite manage it. She looked helplessly at her sister's kind face. Maria pursed her lips and tugged Gwen gently aside into an alcove. Lorena realized they'd fallen behind and came back to join them. "What's going on?"

"Come on, Gwen," Maria urged. "Tell us."

Gwen looked at the carpet. It was a pretty light blue in this part of the room. The color the sky had been on the balcony earlier. She so desperately wanted to get back to how she'd felt on the balcony. "I've just been wondering if . . . if maybe Prince Frederick doesn't like me very much." Her stomach twisted painfully as she said it.

"Oh, Gwennie," Maria said, gathering her into a quick hug. "I don't think it's possible to dislike someone as beautiful inside and out as you." She pulled back and considered. "Prince Frederick does seem a bit shy, though. Maybe you just need to give him a little time."

"That's what I've been trying to believe," Gwen admitted.

"Blaine and Lance are older, and maybe more confident socially," Maria continued. "Frederick seems like he's a little in their shadow. I bet once he feels more comfortable around us, you two will totally hit it off."

"Yeah," Lorena agreed. "He'll come around. He'd better! If

anyone ever makes you feel less than awesome, well, we don't want anything to do with them."

Gwen looked at her sisters gratefully. "Okay. Thanks, Maria. Thanks, Lorena. I'm sure you're right." It was almost true. She *wanted* to be sure they were right. But she wasn't going to ruin this night for them by being gloomy and pessimistic. She made herself smile. "Come on. Let's go find those princes."

It took a while to locate them in the crowd, but they finally spotted the boys near the small stage where Jamie was laid out on top of a neatly made bed. Even now, magically unconscious, Jamie had a faint glow and sparkle about him. A clown in blue and white pinstripes and a pink bunny mask loitered near the set of stairs leading to the stage, handing out balloons. He should have looked jolly, with his fluffy pink ears poking through holes in his tall, pointy clown hat, but the eyes of the mask were sewn as creepy *X*'s, almost as though he were a dead bunny-clown instead of a live one. Gwen avoided letting her gaze linger on him for very long.

Blaine and Frederick seemed to be having a rather heated discussion, and Gwen thought perhaps they should wait to approach, but Lorena, predictably, didn't hesitate.

"Hi, guys!" she said, placing a hand companionably on Frederick's shoulder. "Sorry we had to leave you hanging for a while! What are you talking about?"

Blaine turned to them with a broad smile, the scowl he'd just been directing at Frederick gone as though it had never existed. Frederick just glared at the ground. "We were just observing your kingdom's festivities," Blaine said. "This is all very new to us. Would you mind telling us about what happens at an event like this?"

"Of course," Maria said. "Well, as you can see, people from all over the kingdom have assembled here to attempt to wake Jamie."

Lance had strolled over holding a fresh glass of sparkling cider. "And how do they do that?" he asked.

"Why, with true love's kiss, of course!" Maria said. She nodded at a girl with long, light-brown braids, glasses, and a pretty purple dress who was slowly approaching the stage. "See that brave maiden there? She will kiss Jamie in hopes that an as-yet-unknown love between them will magically wake him."

The girl looked terrified. Her friends were calling out encouragement from the crowd.

"You can do it, Clarissa!"

"Kiss the dreamy prince!"

"Become a Pastel princess!"

Lance tilted his head at the bunny-clown near the stage, who tried, unsuccessfully, to hand the girl a balloon as she walked past. "What's the significance of the clown?"

"No one knows," Lorena whispered ominously.

The girl climbed the stairs and walked over to where Jamie's head was resting on his pillow. Her lips were moving slightly, and Gwen suspected she was giving herself a sotto voce little pep talk.

Chatter in the room died down as everyone waited to see what would happen. Even Frederick was watching with interest now.

The girl leaned down until her face was inches from Jamie's. She hovered there for several long seconds. And then she abruptly straightened back up. "I can't!" she cried. "He's too pretty!"

Then she ran from the stage.

"Well, that didn't work out," Frederick muttered. He glanced around at the other potential kissers waiting for their turn. "I don't think I like this tradition."

The crowd was murmuring again, reacting to the girl's retreat and wondering who would try next. Before anyone could make a move, however, Molly emerged from the wings of the stage and addressed the room. She was holding a covered silver platter.

"Ladies and gentlemen, I'd like to pause our festivities for a moment to thank you all for participating in the wake of Prince James." She lifted the platter's cover to reveal a golden-yellow waffle piled high with whipped cream and chocolate-strawberry topping. "We know that Prince James would have wanted everyone to enjoy his favorite meal with him. Therefore, we'd like to announce that the waffle bar is now open for all guests!"

A cheer went up from the crowd. Molly smiled and began to turn away, only to find the disturbing bunny-clown had crept silently up to stand right beside her. She recoiled with a little yelp of surprise, and the waffle tumbled from the tray and landed toppings-side-down on Jamie's face.

"Oh dear," Molly said mournfully, eyeing the bright-pink and dark-brown syrup that had splattered across Jamie's formerly pristine white shirt.

And then Jamie sat up, his eyes opening wide.

"Oooh!" he said. "Chocolate-strawberry swirl!"

The crowd cheered again, even louder than they had for the waffle-bar announcement.

"Jamie!" Gwen cried, all of her own worries forgotten. She was so relieved to see her brother awake again. Apparently, she'd been more concerned than she'd consciously realized.

"Ha," Lorena said. "True love, indeed."

The girls rushed the stage, joined a second later by their father. "Jamie!" he said. "Thank goodness. Please stop trying to give your poor old dad a heart attack, okay?"

"Okay, Dad," Jamie said. But his voice sounded weak, and he was already lying back down.

Just then the royal medics arrived, and they quickly bundled Jamie off to the infirmary with Molly in tow. Before following them out, King Jack turned back to the guests. "Please, everyone, enjoy yourselves! Eat waffles! Celebrate the regained consciousness of my only son!" Then in a lower voice, he added, "Girls, please stay here for now. I'll be back with an update as soon as I can. Prince Blaine, Prince Lance, Prince Frederick, please excuse me."

"Yes, Father," Maria said, at the same time Blaine said, "Of course, Your Majesty."

Most of the guests had already lined up for waffles. Suddenly the girls found themselves nearly alone in the ballroom with the princes. Even the creepy clown had vanished.

"Welp," Lorena said. "Now you've seen how a wake works!"

"Traditionally, it's supposed to be a kiss from a person," Maria added. "Not a food item."

Gwen smiled. "Jamie doesn't typically go for what's traditional," she said.

"I very much look forward to officially making Prince Jamie's acquaintance," Blaine said. "And I'm finding this glimpse of Pastel Kingdom culture to be completely fascinating."

Maria began to tell him about some of their other unique customs, and Lance asked Lorena what else they did for fun when there wasn't a prince to wake up from a poison-induced slumber. They drifted apart slightly, the older couples deep in conversation, Gwen and Frederick standing in uncomfortable silence.

*Slow-cooked pie,* Gwen reminded herself. Slow-cooked pie wasn't really a thing, unless you meant some kid of meat pie—it was more a technique for, say, brisket—but she knew what she meant. She cleared her throat awkwardly. "Have you been enjoying the party, Prince Frederick?" she asked.

He looked at her, seeming surprised that she had spoken. His eyes met hers, and she noticed again how beautifully green they were—some shade between basil and lime and those cute green lizards that liked to sun themselves on the stones in the royal garden. He opened his mouth, but before he could say anything, her father's voice rang out from the doorway.

"Girls, come with me, please. Jamie is stable for the time being, and the doctor says we can see him briefly if we head over right now." He waved his arms in a hurry-up gesture and disappeared back down the hall.

Maria turned to look at the princes, seeming unsure whether to invite them along.

"Please go ahead," Blaine said smoothly. "And don't worry about us. We don't wish to impose on your limited time with your brother. We'll introduce ourselves after he's had the opportunity to recover." Then he leaned closer to her and added, "But when you're done, I'll be waiting on the balcony to say good night."

Maria's cheeks flared pink as he turned away.

Lance placed a hand on Lorena's shoulder. "If you need me, I'll be gorging myself on waffles for the rest of the evening." Then he trotted off to catch up with Blaine.

Gwen looked around for Frederick, to say she'd see him later, but he was already gone.

Papa was waiting for them just beyond the ballroom.

"I'm glad Jamie woke from the spell so quickly!" Gwen said as they began walking together.

"Yes, me too!" Maria said. "I wonder if there's anything we can bring him."

"Oh!" Gwen exclaimed, suddenly inspired. "I bet Jamie would

appreciate a fresh waffle! The one that woke him ended up in his lap, after all. I know his favorite toppings, I'll go make him one and meet you guys at the infirmary."

"That's a lovely idea, sweetheart," Papa said, kissing her forehead.

"Yes, good thinking!" Lorena added. "You always know the right thing!"

"Take the route through the staff kitchen!" her father called after her. "It's faster!"

"Okay, Papa!" she called back. The staff kitchen suggestion was a good one; it let her avoid all the guests who were now standing around eating their waffles in the ballroom. She ducked through the curtains blocking off the staff entrance and approached the long tables draped with voluminous, pink polka-dotted tablecloths and covered with platters of waffles and everything anyone could ever think of putting on top of a waffle.

She knew just what Jamie would want. She whispered the steps to herself as she worked through them.

"Okay. First, take a waffle and slather it with a hefty amount of strawberries and whipped cream . . . add a second layer and repeat . . . top with a third waffle." She grabbed a knife from the pile of cutlery. "Next, cut a hole all the way down through the center, and fill the hole with a handful of random toppings and sprinkles." She did so, considered, and then added a couple more spoonfuls of sprinkles to be safe. "Lastly, drizzle the whole thing with butterscotch sauce and place a ring of marshmallow bunnies on top." Jamie called this concoction Magical Friendship Volcano Surprise. No one else in the family had ever managed to eat one—the sweetness was overpowering—but Jamie loved it more than anything.

There were four marshmallow bunnies left in the serving bowl, which was exactly what she needed. Perfect! She placed them one by one in a circle around the pit of sprinkles and sauce. They looked like they were playing a little game. Or summoning a tiny demon from a delicious arcane portal.

She was just adjusting the last bunny when it slipped from her fingers and bounced to the carpet underneath the table. "Oh no, I needed that!"

Gwen glanced at the empty bowl, then at the incomplete bunny circle on the waffle monstrosity she'd constructed for Jamie. No, it had to be perfect. She'd just . . . she'd just dust it off really well. The area under the table couldn't be *that* dirty.

She made sure no one was looking and then ducked under the tablecloth.

"Marshmallow bunny," she whisper-sang, "where'd you go?"

She crawled along, overhearing snippets of conversation from the few other people still assembling their waffles. One young woman was complaining about the overabundance of sweets. Someone else was complaining about not having gotten the chance to kiss Jamie before he woke up. Gwen giggled at that one; she couldn't wait to tell Jamie about his disappointed admirers.

Finally, she saw a tiny marshmallow paw underneath a pile of tablecloth fabric where it draped down onto the carpet. "There you are!" she said. She lifted the edge of the tablecloth to reveal the elusive bunny just as she realized the voices she could hear now were familiar. Was that—yes, it was Frederick and Blaine. She looked up, her head now sticking out from under the tablecloth just enough so that she could see them. They weren't standing as close to the table as those other people had been, so she hadn't been able to make out what they were saying before. They were arguing. Again. Their voices had been quiet but were growing louder.

"Frederick, lower your voice!" Blaine hissed.

But Frederick wasn't listening to his brother. His voice had risen to where it was impossible for her not to hear. Especially since the next word was her own name.

"Gwendolyn," he was saying, his voice twisted with some emotion she could not identify, "is *really ugly!*"

# CHAPTER 6
## GWENDOLYN

Very slowly and very quietly, Gwen backed away from the princes, sliding back underneath the table. She let the tablecloth fall back into place, hiding her from view. They hadn't seen her. That was good. It would seem pretty strange that she was crawling around under the waffle bar. Of course it would. It wasn't exactly normal behavior. What was she doing down here again?

She found herself looking at the marshmallow bunny she now held in one hand. Right. She was making a waffle for Jamie. She'd needed this last little guy for the mini waffle-top tableau. Well. Now she had him. She should go.

She crawled back to the far end of the table, slipping silently out and getting to her feet. She grabbed the plate with Jamie's waffle and then ducked back through the curtains to the kitchen. As she walked, she pressed the last bunny carefully into his place in the circle with the others. *There you go*, she thought. *Right where you belong.*

Her head felt weirdly empty as she walked down one hallway after another. Usually her mind felt full of all kinds of thoughts, all the time, but now she wasn't thinking about anything at all.

She was standing outside the infirmary door. How long had she been standing there? She could hear her family's voices on the other side. She pushed the door open.

"Hello?" she said, stepping inside.

"Gwennie!" Jamie shouted. He flashed her a radiant smile.

"Jamie, I'm so glad you're okay." She stepped closer. "I made you your favorite."

Jamie thrust his arms into the air with excitement. "Magical Friendship Volcano Surprise!"

"Ugh," Lorena said, wrinkling her nose. "I don't know how you can eat those things."

"It can't be good for you," Maria added. "Anyway, you're already sweet enough!"

"Now, girls, Jamie's had a rough day," Papa said. "I think he deserves a disgusting waffle tower if he wants one."

The good-natured teasing should have made Gwen want to join in, but somehow it made her feel even more alone. And she couldn't let them see anything was wrong. This was a happy occasion. Jamie was recovering, her sisters had had a wonderful evening, and her father was pleased. If they saw she was upset, they would want to know why. They would ask her and they wouldn't take no for an answer and she couldn't—she didn't want to—no, she couldn't stay. She had to leave. Right now.

"Um, so actually," she said, not quite looking at any of them, "I was thinking of heading to bed now. I'm feeling pretty sleepy."

"Of course, cutie-pie," Papa said at once. "It's been a really long day, hasn't it? And so much excitement. You go get some rest."

"Thank you, Papa," Gwen said. She turned to go.

Then he said, "Just be sure to say a proper goodbye to the Plaid princes first, okay?"

She stopped, took a breath. "Um, sure. Yes, Papa." She made herself smile. "Good night, everyone."

"Sweet dreams, Gwen!" Maria said.

"See you in the morning!" Lorena said.

"Mmmmmmph-mmmph," Jamie added, his mouth full of Magical Friendship Volcano Surprise. He waved his fork at her.

Gwen stepped into the hall and closed the door behind her.

Distantly, she could hear the sounds of the party still going on. There was music playing now, and the faint buzzing and chiming of the game booths where guests could try to win prizes, and the soft bleating of the sheep in the petting zoo, and underneath it all, the constant low rumble of conversation. All she had to do was walk down this hall, then turn right and walk down another hall, and she'd eventually run into the princes. Blaine and Frederick had probably stopped arguing by now. Blaine was probably getting ready to go wait for Maria on the balcony like he'd promised. Lance was probably eating more waffles. And Frederick—

Gwen started walking in the other direction. Away from the ballroom. Away from everything.

*What am I doing?* She didn't know. She still wasn't really thinking coherent thoughts. She just knew she couldn't face the princes. She couldn't. She had to get away.

She was running now. She ran down the stairs and then out the side entrance, the small door that would never be used by guests. She ran out into the cool night, still with no idea where she was headed. She just needed to run.

She'd always thought that all princesses, by nature, were beautiful. That it was just part of being a princess. She had never questioned it. Her family always told her she was beautiful. Of course, she could see that she wasn't beautiful in the same way her sisters were, or that Jamie was. But she'd always liked what she'd seen in the mirror. She thought she was just beautiful in her own, unique way. She hadn't realized—she'd thought—

She'd also always assumed that all princesses would meet their Prince Charmings and fall in love instantly. Since this afternoon, she'd been trying to tell herself that wasn't how it really worked, that those things took time, but it certainly seemed to be happening for the others. Maria and Lorena were completely smitten, and

Blaine and Lance seemed equally enraptured. *Not me, though. Not Frederick. And now I know why.*

She'd been so stupid.

*Slow pie.* What a joke. Frederick wasn't any kind of pie. Or if he was, he wasn't going to be *her* pie. They would never be or have or create any kind of pie together. Her whole pie metaphor was crumbling apart, destroyed like Frederick had destroyed his slice of apple pie earlier. It had been a ridiculous metaphor to begin with anyway. Ridiculous, like her.

She was crying now, and the tears blurred her vision. She didn't even know where she was. She'd never been more than a few steps from the palace before. It was dark, and there were trees—oh god, had she run right into the haunted forest?

They were never supposed to go into the haunted forest. Not ever. She and her sisters were never supposed to go *anywhere*, but especially not the haunted forest. There were things in the forest that no one understood. Horrible sounds, terrifying shapes . . . she had heard one rumor about unearthly howls that erupted from the depths of the forest once a month at midnight. Howls like no human or animal could ever make. Even the guards were afraid to go into the forest, especially after dark. She had to turn around, go back . . . except, she wasn't even sure which way *was* back anymore.

She made herself stand still, trying to listen past the sound of her own ragged breathing. All around her, huge trees stretched up into the night, their branches seeming to claw angrily at the sky. If there was any kind of a path, she couldn't see it. Everything around her was blackness and shadow.

But—wait—was that a light in the distance? That must be the palace. Weak with relief, she ran toward it, stumbling over roots and rocks. She'd sneak inside and go right to bed. The party would still be in full swing. She didn't have to talk to anyone. She just had to get back.

Then she heard something in the darkness behind her.

She stopped again, breathing hard, trying to listen. Yes—there—rustling in the leaves, hushed whispers. She whirled around.

Five terrifying figures stood facing her in the sudden silence. With the tree-filtered moonlight behind them they were nothing more than shadow-black silhouettes arranged across the path, but their eyes glowed like torches.

"Oh my god," Gwen whispered, stumbling backward. Then she screamed, "Help! Someone, please!"

She turned and ran once more, flying over the uneven ground as fast as she could. When she risked a glance back over her shoulder, she saw the figures closing the distance. "No! Please, stay away!"

Taking her eyes of the ground as she ran had been a mistake. Her ankle struck a log, and she fell hard to the dirt, screaming again with the pain. She scrambled onto her back, watching in terror as the figures came closer. Her heart felt like it was trying to climb right out of her chest. *I'm going to die here*, she thought frantically. *Alone in the darkness, away from my family.* She tried to send her love to them through the night. *I'm sorry. I love you. I'm so thankful for every day I got to spend with you!*

But then, maybe this was for the best. They had the princes now. She would just have been in the way. She didn't want to believe that, but she feared it was true. Without her, Maria and Lorena would be free to marry Blaine and Lance. Frederick would be free to find himself the beautiful girl he wanted. They were better off without her complicating all of their lives.

One of the figures reached a long appendage toward her, and it was finally all too much. The world went blurry around the edges, then black.

# CHAPTER 7
## GWENDOLYN

Gwen blinked awake, sunlight flickering against her eyes. Then she gasped and sat up, the events of the previous night slamming back into her mind. She was—alive?! How? And—where?

Her dress had been replaced with an unfamiliar lacy nightgown, and her right arm had a clean bandage tied neatly around it at the elbow. She must have scraped it when she fell. *But who—?*

She surveyed the room. She was wrapped in a soft, pink blanket on a velvety love seat in someone's living room. The furniture was elegant and tasteful, and there were fresh flowers in vases on various surfaces. She became aware of murmuring voices, and when she turned to look, she saw that the living room doors opened onto a pretty garden patio where several young women sat around a table. She couldn't see their faces, but some had delicate crowns atop their neatly styled hair, and all of them wore lovely dresses. Gwen got unsteadily to her feet. Her shoes were lined up neatly beside the love seat, and she slipped into them, in case she had to run.

One of the women caught sight of her. "She's awake!" the stranger said in a low voice to her companions. Then they were all staring and whispering. Why—? But then she remembered. She heard Frederick's words, as though he were standing right behind her: *Gwendolyn is really ugly.*

Gwen wanted to dive back under the blanket. The women on the patio all seemed to be beautiful, glamorous princesses of some kind. They were probably whispering about how she looked. About how ugly she was.

"Uh, hey there, kiddo," someone said. Gwen felt a gentle hand on her shoulder. "Sorry about last night."

Gwen turned to see a tall, striking woman in maybe her mid-twenties. She wore a black pantsuit with a blue bodice under the jacket and gold polygon symbols on each shoulder. A tiara with five black spikes emerging from three gold polygons rested on her steel-blue hair.

"Huh? Wh—what do you mean?"

"I think we may have accidentally given you a scare when you ran into us in the forest. You took a tumble and fainted. We, um—well, we can't be too careful, and we can't assume anyone wandering through these parts at night is necessarily friendly. But once we saw that you weren't a threat, we brought you here and patched you up."

The monstrous figures in the forest—had been these women? It had been so dark, and she'd been so upset . . . she supposed it was possible. Humiliating, but possible. And it was certainly better to be embarrassed than dead.

Gwen dipped her head and curtsied as well as she could in just a nightgown. "Thank you for treating my wounds and letting me stay the night," she said. "I'm so sorry to have been a bother. Please let me know how I can ever repay you."

The blue-haired woman smiled. "Well, aren't you the most polite little vagabond we've ever met!"

"Vagabond! What? No—I'm a princess, just like you all seem to be!" She hesitated, some of her indignation falling away. "Though apparently I may not look it . . ."

The woman blinked, clearly startled. "A princess? Just like us?" She slapped a hand to her forehead. "Of course! How could we not notice?" She put an arm around Gwen's shoulders and turned her to face the others, who had been watching their exchange from the patio. "Hey, everyone! She's one of us! You don't have to worry—come say hello!"

That seemed an odd thing to say. Why would they have been worried? But then, proper princesses probably didn't want to associate with ugly vagabonds. The others began to rise from their chairs, making various positive exclamations that didn't seem quite in line with the situation.

"Oh, thank goodness!"

"That's wonderful news!"

Then they all came toward her in a rush, and Gwen had to resist the urge to step backward as she was surrounded by a rustle of fabric and enthusiastic voices. A woman with long, wavy, brown hair swept up in a high ponytail took Gwen by the shoulders and guided her to a chair at a round dining table. "It's so nice to meet you! Have a seat. And please, have some wine!" She produced a bottle of white wine from—somewhere—and poured it into a glass that had also suddenly materialized.

"Um, no thanks," Gwen told her, trying to hide her discomfort. "I'm only sixteen. Also, isn't it . . . very early in the morning?"

Just then a crow flew in through an open window. No one else seemed to find this unusual, so Gwen didn't say anything. But then the crow landed on the seat beside her and with a loud *poof* transformed into a young woman with long black hair and round, gold glasses.

Gwen's mouth fell open. *Did that just happen?*

"Hii!" the young woman said. "I'm sooooo relieved!"

"R-relieved? I don't—"

"No, no, no," a new voice broke in. Gwen turned away from the crow-girl—*crow-girl?!*—to see an elegant woman slightly older than the others, with red hair swept up into a formal bun. "Do not serve this poor girl this wine! Honestly, you ought to know better."

*Finally,* Gwen thought. *A voice of reason in all this chaos.*

"When it comes to wine," the woman continued, "redder is better!" She then lifted an expensive-looking bottle of red wine in two enormous lobster claws. Gwen blinked, at first thinking the claws were some kind of elaborate gloves—or oven mitts?—but no . . . no, those were her hands. Why were those her hands? What the heck was this place? Maybe she *had* been right to be terrified.

"Hello," a new voice said. Gwen turned again, feeling like she was getting whiplash. The crow-girl was gone, and now a new girl sat in her place. "I'm Princess Jolie of the Lace Kingdom. I hope you don't mind—I changed you into one of my nightgowns after you fell last night." This girl, at least, looked like a regular normal human person. She seemed to be just a year or two older than Maria, and she had pretty gray hair and bright pink eyes.

"Oh, thank you so much," Gwen said, feeling genuine gratitude (as well as relief that this girl didn't seem to be part animal in any way). "That was very kind of you."

"Of course!" Princess Jolie said. "We're so happy to have another friend in our club who understands who we truly are."

Gwen had no idea what she was talking about. What club? Did this girl also have something strange about her? She seemed so normal, though.

"Oh," Gwen said, suddenly noticing a speck of something in

Jolie's eye. "I think you have something in your eye. An eyelash, maybe?"

"Oh, really? Ugh, it's probably lint. Thank you for letting me know." Then she pulled up the mask that she had apparently been wearing—a mask that had those pretty pink eyes on it—to reveal huge gaping black holes where her actual eyes should be.

Gwen stared, trying not to scream.

Just then, the first woman tapped a spoon against her wine glass—did they all drink wine before breakfast in this place?—to get everyone's attention. "It's about time we begin today's club meeting."

"Oh," Gwen said, "I should go. I don't want to intrude." *I should definitely go. Very quickly. Before anything else terrifying happens.* She started to stand up.

"No, no—you should stay," the blue-haired woman said, motioning for Gwen to sit back down. "Maybe you'll want to join! And we should all introduce ourselves. My name is Princess Calpernia of the Polygon Kingdom. I'm the founder and president of the club."

"We all call her Prez," whispered the crow-girl, who had reappeared behind Gwen's chair.

"Nice to meet you," Gwen said, "but I really should—"

"And I'd love to introduce you to the other girls," Princess Calpernia said. "But, um, I don't know your name."

"Oh! How rude of me," Gwen said. Reluctantly, she sat down

again. This whole situation was so bizarre, she had completely forgotten her manners. No matter what else had happened, she was still a representative of her family and should comport herself accordingly. "I'm Princess Gwendolyn of the Pastel Kingdom. But I'm afraid I still don't understand what this club of yours is, or why you'd want me to join."

Princess Calpernia winked at her. "Let me give you the official spiel. You're familiar with fairy tales, right, Gwendolyn?"

"Yes, my whole family loves them," Gwen said. Princess Calpernia's straightforward demeanor and lack of obvious horrific qualities was making her feel slightly more relaxed. And she did love a good story.

"Well, then, as you know, in your typical fairy tale, princesses often face difficult perils—for example, Sleeping Beauty and the spinning wheel's sharp spindle—and become cursed with an affliction. In SB's case, a magical sleep."

Gwen nearly laughed. "Oh, yes, I'm *very* familiar with that one."

"In the stories, the curse is always broken just in time, and the princess wins a happily-ever-after with her Prince Charming. But in real life, it's not always that simple. You never read about the princesses whose curses don't get mended completely, or about when there aren't any known remedies for their curse."

"Does that happen?" Gwen asked. "I thought—"

"Of course you did," Princess Calpernia said, pointing at Gwen for emphasis. "Because that's what the stories tell you.

They also *don't* tell you what happens to those unlucky princesses when—well, ladies, what unattainably high expectations does society have for princesses?"

The others called out responses.

"That we always look young and beautiful!"

"That we live perfect, inspirational lives!"

"That we have fingers!"

Princess Calpernia nodded gravely. "So we, the cursed princesses, are hidden or even locked away by our families, unfit to represent our kingdoms. And the notion of a Prince Charming or a happily ever after quickly fades away forever."

Around the room, several of the other girls murmured unhappy agreement.

*Cursed princesses.* Gwen felt the last of her fear giving way to sympathy. That would explain the frightening deformities and strange abilities the other young women had demonstrated. How awful that must be for them! But some of them looked perfectly normal. What could their curses be?

"So," Calpernia continued, "I decided to take one of my family's old vacation homes—which, um, happened to be located in your quaint kingdom, please don't tell your dad—and turn it into a secret sanctuary that the cursed princesses can escape to. I want this to be a place where we can support one another and remind ourselves that we are still beautiful and worthy of happiness, no matter what any person or prince thinks!"

"But mostly it's a place where we eat junk food and escape from the world," the crow-girl added.

"Okay, so there's still room for improvement," Calpernia said. "But I think we're doing pretty great so far." She spread her hands. "Anyway, welcome to Cursed Princess Club Headquarters!

"Thank you for explaining," Gwen said, starting to get up again. "But I should really—"

"Now let's all go around and introduce ourselves and our curses!"

Gwen sank back into the chair. She did want to leave, but she didn't want to offend all of these other princesses. At least she no longer felt the need to flee for her life. Everything had taken on a far less ominous cast now that she knew these women were victims, not villains. Assuming she could believe them, of course. But her heart was telling her that Princess Calpernia was telling the truth. And besides, if they'd wanted to hurt her, they could have done so quite easily while she was unconscious. Instead, they'd helped her. They'd shown her nothing but kindness since she'd awakened. She would not repay that kindness with unwarranted suspicion. She would stay for the introductions, and then she would ask them to excuse her so she could head home.

"Who wants to go first?" Calpernia asked. "Monika? How about you?"

The crow-girl—Monika, apparently—spit out the sip of wine she'd just taken. "M-me? B-but—um, okay." She took a deep breath.

"My name is Princess Monika of the Quilt Kingdom. When I was little, I was taken hostage by an evil wizard who turned me into his pet crow. He was defeated eventually, and I was turned human again. But for some reason, I still transform into a crow when I get, um . . . um . . ." She looked apologetically at Gwen. "Sorry, I hate talking in front of people. Um . . . when I get . . . anxious."

There was another *poof*, and then the crow was back, standing on the table. It gave a little hop and then tried to stick its beak in the wine glass.

"Excellent!" said Calpernia. "Who's next?"

"I guess I'll go next," said a girl who was standing on the other side of the table, facing slightly away. She had pretty, aquamarine hair and wore a cute, brightly-colored jacket with an equally colorful backpack. "I have to head out soon and start my homework anyway."

*She looks like she might be about my age!* Gwen thought. The other young women all seemed to be at least a few years older. Even though she'd already decided she had no interest in joining this strange club, her heart leapt a little at the idea of making a friend her own age. She'd never had one before.

But then the girl turned around and smiled with the wrinkled face of an old lady. "Hi, Gwendolyn," she said. "I'm Princess Abbi of the Neon Kingdom. I'm fifteen."

*Huh*, Gwen thought, unable to think of what to say. *I guess she's actually a little younger than me, then.*

"Several months ago I was given a box that would supposedly give me everlasting happiness as long as I didn't open it. So, uh, yeah. I opened it. And now I look like an old lady, and the doctors say there's no cure. It sucks. This guy Bobby that I like was just about to ask me out, too, but now he's just, like, really respectful to me."

"Great, thanks, Abbi," Calpernia said. "Saffron, why don't you go next?"

"Sounds good. Hey, I'm Saffron from the Foliage Kingdom." This princess had a super deep voice, and Gwen was startled by her less-than-feminine features. Then she felt both ashamed of herself for being judgy and humbled by the open-mindedness of the club members, who clearly embraced their diverse looks confidently and wholeheartedly.

Saffron's eyes narrowed. "Stop looking at me like that! I know that look! I'm not a princess, I'm a man!"

"Oh," Gwen said. "I—I can see that. I'm sorry."

"Ah, right," Calpernia put in. "I should mention that we have some male members. Well, one. But the name Cursed Princess Club was already well established, so we just never changed it. I mean, I had already printed up T-shirts and stuff."

"I hate it!" Saffron said. "You need to change it!"

The blue-haired woman rolled her eyes. "Just hurry up and say what your curse is."

"Ugh, okay." He grew serious, his voice low and grim. "My

curse is that I can't grow a full, majestic beard like all the other men in my royal lineage. It's a horrible, despicable curse."

"That's not what your curse is," Calpernia said.

"Ughhh, fiiiiiine!" Saffron held up his left hand, which was green and scaly with pointy claws instead of fingers. "I guess I also have this evil hand that a goblin cursed me with? I can't control its movements, and it terrorizes people around me. But it's really not that bad. Not like the beard thing."

"So what's your curse, Gwendolyn?" Monika—who had unbirded again—asked.

Gwen blinked. "What? No, I don't—"

"Ooh, let us guess!" she interrupted, clapping her hands excitedly.

"Did you switch bodies with a witch?" Abbi asked.

Gwen stared at her. "No! Is—is that what I look like?" *Is that what Frederick thought too?*

"I know," Saffron said. "Were you an old mop that got brought to life? I've got a buddy who used to be barbecue tongs."

"What? No!" *Oh my god.* She must be even uglier than she'd realized. An old *mop*?!

"Were you—" Monika began.

"Stop!" Gwen shouted. "I don't have a curse! This is—this is just how I've always looked. I didn't know—I didn't mean to join your cursed princess club. I just accidentally stumbled here after a bad night. I'm sorry." She was *not* going to cry. She was not. But she couldn't meet anyone's eyes either.

"Oh, whoops," Saffron said. Monika *poof*ed into a crow again.

"Prez, do something," Abbi said.

Calpernia pressed a hand to her forehead. "How do you guys keep thinking that guessing game is a good idea?" She sighed. "But I'm the one who first assumed she had a curse, so it's really my fault. I'm sorry, Gwendolyn. We're so used to everyone here being cursed, we just never questioned that you must have a curse too. I hope you can forgive us." A tiny bell chimed, and Calpernia took a fancy pocket watch out of her jacket. "Oh, hey, look! It's eight o'clock, which means it's time for morning affirmations! Gwendolyn, please join us. They're really uplifting."

Gwen gasped. "It's eight o'clock already?" She stood up and backed away from the table. "I have to get home before my family wakes up and realizes I was out all night!"

Calpernia stood up too. "Oh, sure, okay. We understand. But hey, kiddo—why don't you come back sometime? I can't help but think there's something on your mind that our little club could maybe help with." She scowled momentarily at the others. "Despite the idiotic things we do sometimes."

"Yeah, please come back!" Abbi said. "We'll make it up to you!"

"We didn't even finish the introductions," Monika said.

Gwen paused. "Really? Even though I don't have a curse?"

"I mean, it's practically one," Abbi said.

"A minor technicality, really," said Monika.

"Um, yeah. I'd say you're good," Calpernia added.

Right. Gwen felt all the crushing despair of yesterday settling back over her like a shroud. "I think I'll pass."

"Tell ya what," Calpernia said, walking her to the door. "We'll send you an invitation, and you can think about it. But please don't tell anyone about our location, okay? It's really important that we have a secret place here that's just our own. I think you can understand."

"Yes," Gwen said. "I won't. And thank you again for taking care of me last night, everyone." Then she turned and ran back into the forest.

# CHAPTER 8

## GWENDOLYN

The forest was much less scary in the daylight. Now the giant trees seemed to be reaching up to welcome the sun, and there were pretty flowers scattered among the roots. There was even a very clear path, now that she could see well enough to look for it.

Gwen walked quickly, not wanting to risk running since there were still rocks and things she could trip over. She wished she'd thought to change back into her dress before she left. At least she had her shoes! The long walk would have been very uncomfortable without them. And luckily the nightgown was a fairly modest one. She'd have to figure out how to get inside unseen once she reached the palace, though. Modest or not, she didn't usually go wandering outside in her pajamas, and she definitely did not want to invite any awkward questions. She'd also have to figure out how to get the nightgown back to Jolie at some point.

Was she really going to consider going back to that house? Joining their strange club? For a moment, when they'd all been urging her to return, she'd been tempted. Once she'd gotten past her initial fright, the girls—and Saffron—had all been so friendly and welcoming. The idea of having new friends, not just one but a whole slew of them, was extremely enticing. She loved her family beyond anything, but she and her sisters had always been so sheltered and isolated. Jamie got to travel around for his food critic business, but the rest of them had been confined to the palace for their entire lives. Well, except for Maria's occasional sneaking out to buy things from local stores. Gwen had never figured out how Maria managed that without getting caught.

She understood Papa's reasons—well, kind of—and she knew he was only trying to protect them. And his restrictions, while frustrating, had been bearable because she and her siblings had always had each other. But now her sisters would be spending more and more time with Blaine and Lance. And eventually getting married to them. Which would leave Gwen much more alone, since obviously Frederick had no interest in marrying her. He'd probably already told his father to call off the engagement. And it wasn't like she wanted to marry him anymore, either, after what he'd said. Just the thought of it made her want to curl up somewhere in the dark and cry. Or throw up. Or both.

She kicked a rock from the path, trying to get her feelings back under control. She didn't have to think about what Frederick had said if she didn't want to. But whether she thought about it or not, the consequences would be the same. She and Maria and Lorena had sworn just yesterday—had it only been *yesterday?*—that they would always stay close, but that didn't mean they would still see each other every day like they did now. At least one of her sisters would probably end up moving to the Plaid Kingdom. It had seemed manageable when she thought they'd all be entering the new world of married life together, but now Gwen couldn't help but fear there would be a new divide between them. They'd be moving on, and she'd be left behind.

If she joined the club . . . well, it couldn't replace her family, of course, but at least she'd have some new friends to talk to and spend time with. She hadn't met all the club members yet, but she had liked the ones she'd met so far. Monika was sweet, Jolie was kind, Saffron was funny, and Princess Calpernia seemed very dedicated to looking after everyone else.

But then she remembered all of their guesses about her "curse." Did she really want to join a group that believed her appearance was so awful that there had to be evil magic behind it? Frederick's words had made her feel worse than she ever had in her life, but the club's assumptions only seemed to confirm that what he said had been true. She really was ugly. It wasn't just Frederick's opinion. It was a fact. Maybe her family just loved her too much to see the truth, but it was glaringly obvious to everyone else.

Gwen had barely been paying attention to where she was walking, but her feet must have remembered the way, because the familiar colors of the Pastel Palace were glinting prettily at her through the few remaining rows of trees. She stopped, still deep enough in the forest's cover to be invisible to anyone who might be looking in her direction. Now, how was she going to get in without causing a scene? Standing there studying the grounds, a plan suddenly came to her. She dashed out from under the trees and swerved into the royal garden. Then she plucked a quick bunch of yellow wildflowers and headed inside.

Hopefully her family would still be asleep, but at least now she had a story ready, just in case. The servants probably wouldn't challenge her, but she was grateful not to see any of them about either. She ran through the empty hallways and up the stairs. And then jerked to a halt, nearly dropping her flowers.

Papa was outside her room, having a complete meltdown.

"Guards! My baby's been kidnapped!" He was shouting and pacing, clawing his fingers into the sides of his face in his panic. "Deploy all troops and artillery immediately! *Who took my baby girl?*"

"P-Papa?"

He turned and deflated instantly, then rushed to her and folded her into his arms. "Gwen! Oh, thank goodness. Where were you, sweetie?" Belatedly, he called over his shoulder, "Uh, stand down, guards! Sorry! My bad!"

"I woke up early this morning, so I went out and gathered some wildflowers from the garden." She held up her handful of flowers as evidence. *I can't believe I'm lying to Papa! I'm sorry!*

He chuckled fondly. "Ooh, my little early bird! It's just like you to do something adorable like that! You had me worried, though." He held her out at arm's length and looked at her. "Don't scare Papa that way. Oh, that's also an adorable new nightgown!" Then, suddenly, he frowned and pointed at her. "Wait a second!"

*Oh god, he knows I'm lying!*

He grabbed her wrist. "Is that a bandage? Did you hurt your arm? What happened?"

She couldn't let him know she'd been off the palace grounds. "I—I think I accidentally caught it on my possum's claws while I was sleeping. It's very minor!"

Her father's face was cold with fury as he leaned into the open door of her bedroom and glared at Mr. Possum. "If this leaves a scar, I will personally rip out every nail and tooth from your vile body," he said in a terrifying whisper.

"Papa, no—it's nothing, I swear!" *I'm sorry, Mr. Possum! I'll bring you extra treats for a month!*

"Morning, Gwen!" It was Lorena, with Maria walking beside her. Gwen didn't think she'd ever been more relieved to see her sisters. "How'd ya sleep last night?"

Papa, his anger gone as quickly as it had appeared, smiled around at all of them. "I'll go put these pretty flowers in some water and leave you to your girl talk." He practically skipped away down the hall.

"Oh, um, I slept pretty well," Gwen said. "So what did I miss after I went to bed last night?"

"Nothing big," Maria said, but her face went all dreamy and she lifted a hand to touch her cheek without seeming to realize it. "I just talked with Blaine about music on the balcony for a while. Do you know he likes Schozart almost as much as I do? And he plays the piano! He's going to learn the accompaniment to *The Magic Sousaphone* so we can perform it together!"

"That's so great!" Gwen said. "How about you, Lorena?"

Now it was Lorena's turn to get dreamy faced. "Well, I went to the waffle bar after we left Jamie at the infirmary, and Lance was there on like his tenth one or something, but anyway he'd made me a waffle! It had strawberries and butterscotch and he'd written *I think you're waffle-y cool* in blueberry syrup. I mean, so goofy, right? But also so charming and sweet. And man, the way he can pack away food is *super* sexy."

Gwen laughed. "That sounds perfect! Oh, I'm so glad you two had such a good night."

"Well, what about you, Gwen?" Maria asked, poking her playfully in the arm. "Did you get to talk to Frederick more? Are you looking forward to seeing him again?"

"Huh? Oh, um . . ." Gwen struggled to keep smiling. She *never* wanted to see Frederick again. Not ever. But she couldn't tell them that. "Yes, of course. That would be wonderful." She swallowed, hard. "Hey, were you guys headed down to breakfast? I'll go get changed and meet you there."

"Oh, okay!" Maria said. "We'll see you downstairs, then."

Gwen ducked into her room and closed the door behind her. She sat on the bed, and Mr. Possum and Mr. Rat scurried over, wanting comfort after being yelled at by the king. Gwen pulled them gently into her lap and ran her fingers through their soft fur. She needed some comfort herself. She'd never thought she would keep secrets from her sisters. Not about anything. But if they found out what Frederick had said about her, they would defend her at all costs. Even it meant cutting things off with the Plaid princes entirely.

She couldn't let that happen. Her sisters were so happy. They and the older princes were perfect for each other. She wasn't going to ruin that just because she was—because she wasn't—

Hot tears began to squeeze out of her eyes, and she swiped at them angrily. She couldn't fall apart. She had to get dressed and go down to breakfast and pretend that everything was fine. But how long would she have to keep pretending? And what about the next time they were supposed to see the princes? Surely her sisters would want to invite them back as soon as possible. Her father too. What was she going to do?

Unbidden, the image of Princess Calpernia reappeared in her mind. *Hey, kiddo—why don't you come back sometime? I can't help but think there's something on your mind that our little club could maybe help with.*

It had been a kind offer, but how could they possibly help her? And anyway, the more she considered it, the less she thought she'd ever be desperate enough to go back to that place. Kind or not, collectively all those troubled princesses—and Saffron—might just be too much. And she didn't know how to get past the idea that they all thought she had been cursed to look the way she did. Wouldn't she just be reminded of that every time they looked at her?

No. She would just have to figure something out on her own. Some perfect solution that allowed her sisters to go on and be happy without her, that helped them accept that she wasn't going to be married along with them. But then another horrible thought occurred to her. She stopped petting her animals. She seemed to have lost the ability to move. She was barely able to breathe.

What if Frederick *hadn't* asked his father to call off the engagement? What if he was planning to go through with the marriage, as his princely duty, even though he found her repulsive? As hurt and disappointed as she was by everything that had happened, the idea of still having to be around Frederick, to spend the rest of her *life* with him, was far, far, worse. She realized she'd been assuming since last night that he would simply refuse the match. But if he didn't . . . if he didn't, then *Gwen* would have to be the one to refuse. And how could she explain her reasons to her family without telling them the truth? Which she couldn't ever tell them, because it would taint her sisters' happiness and ruin everything?

Gwen flopped back on the bed and stared at the ceiling, ignoring Mr. Possum's and Mr. Rat's squeaky pleas for continued petting. She felt like she was caught in a trap with no way to escape. But, no, there had to be a way out. There was always a solution, if you just kept looking for it. Wasn't there? She thought of Calpernia's explanation about the origins of the club, and how some curses could never be cured. But that was different. This wasn't a curse. This was her life. She wasn't going to just give up.

She got out of bed and began to get dressed, grabbing a random dress from her wardrobe and slipping the nightgown off over her head. She was going to pull herself together and eat some breakfast and believe that she would figure something out.

Somehow.

# CHAPTER 9

## FREDERICK

Frederick pulled the covers over his head, trying to ignore the insistent knocking on his bedroom door.

"Go away," he said into his pillow.

The knocking got louder. It was more like pounding now. And from the relentless force and apparently tireless repetition, he could only assume the knocker was Lance. That was unfortunate. Lance was never going to go away until he got what he wanted.

"Ughhh," Frederick said, sitting up. His face hurt. Why did his face hurt?

Oh. Now he remembered. Blaine had slapped him. Slapped him! Right in front of the Pastel Palace waffle bar!

He scowled, but that made his face hurt more, so he stopped

doing that and settled for clenching his fists instead. Who did Blaine think he was?

Everything about the previous day and night had been awful. Frederick thought he'd been doing a masterful job of keeping up appearances, but inside he'd been seething. And after Prince Jamie woke up, and the king and his daughters left to see him in the infirmary, Frederick just hadn't been able to pretend anymore. And he shouldn't have had to pretend! Not when he was just talking to his brother! But when he told Blaine he wanted to go home, Blaine had completely flipped out.

"What is your problem today?!" he'd demanded, grabbing Frederick's wrist.

"My problem?!" Frederick couldn't even believe Blaine needed to ask. "My *problem* is that you and Lance got beautiful fiancés, and I got the short end of the stick!"

"What are you talking about? We all saw their portrait beforehand, and you were the most excited!"

"Well, yeah, I know, but that was because of the portrait, remember? We all thought Prince Jamie was a princess!"

Blaine crossed his arms. "I most certainly did not."

Frederick nearly lost his mind at that. "Why are you lying?! I know you thought he was the youngest princess when we looked at the portrait, and then again when we saw him in person! You and Lance were *entranced* by him!"

"Mm, no, I have no idea what you're talking about."

It took all of Frederick's strength not to claw Blaine's eyes out right then. They had all thought Jamie was the princess. They had. And now Blaine was pretending that they had known the third princess was that horrible witchy-looking girl all along. With effort, Frederick resisted digging his fingernails into his brother's stupid face and limited himself to verbally assaulting him with all the best swear words he could think of.

"Compose yourself, Frederick!"

"Compose this, you jerk!" Okay, that hadn't been his best comeback ever, but he was so mad that he could barely think straight.

Blaine made himself all extra tall and straight-backed in that self-righteous posture he always took on when he was going to be extra insufferable. "So then is the issue that you'd prefer to be courting Prince Jamie? Because we can see if that could be arranged."

"What? No, of course not! I don't like boys that way, and you know it! I'm not going to date a prince, Blaine!"

"Well, then, Gwen is a lovely alternative."

"No, she's not! She's not lovely and you know that too!" He was shouting now, and some part of him knew that wasn't the best idea given that they were arguing in public, but he couldn't seem to help it. He was so angry. Angry and disappointed and feeling entirely sorry for himself. And his own brother wouldn't even acknowledge what was really happening! "For once, just get off your high horse and admit it! *Admit it!*"

"Frederick," Blaine said, his voice getting a dangerous edge, "lower your voice."

But Frederick couldn't make himself stop. All his shock and sadness and anger was pouring out of him now like a raging river. "She looks nothing like the rest of her family! They're all insanely beautiful! But Gwendolyn—Gwendolyn is . . . Gwendolyn is *really ugly*!"

And then Blaine had slapped him hard enough to make him stumble back against the wall.

"How *dare* you speak such horrid words!" Blaine's face was deathly serious and full of fury. "Father will be hearing about all of this."

Then he'd stormed away, leaving Frederick standing there holding his face and afraid to look around to see if anyone had noticed. They hadn't spoken for the rest of the night, not even on the carriage ride home.

And now Frederick guessed he would have to face him. Face all of them. Lance was still out there knocking.

He supposed he had acted a bit inappropriately. He certainly shouldn't have been shouting like that in the Pastel Palace ballroom. And his words had been . . . well, pretty harsh, in retrospect. But it wasn't like Gwendolyn had *heard* him or anything. The whole family had been in the infirmary. And he should be able to be honest with his own brother! But he'd be honest more quietly, next time, for sure.

"Come in, already!" he called at the door.

Lance opened it and stepped through immediately. At least he didn't just barge in without being invited. That was one nice thing about Lance—he could be a jerk, like a *lot*, but he respected boundaries.

"Morning, li'l bro. Dad wanted me to come get you for breakfast and to tell you that he's—let me quote him exactly here—royally pissed."

Frederick swallowed nervously. Father was scary even when he was in a good mood. This was not going to be pleasant.

"How's your face?" Lance waved a finger in the general direction of Frederick's right cheek.

"It's fine," Frederick lied. "Barely felt it."

Lance smirked. "Ha—I'll tell Blaine to put his back into it next time. But, um, maybe play nice today, huh? You're already gonna have Dad on your case pretty hard."

"Yeah. Yeah, okay. Thanks, Lance."

"I'll wait in the hall while you get dressed. Dad said not to come back without you." He ducked back out and closed the door behind him.

Frederick swapped his green plaid pajamas for the green plaid uniform his father insisted on and ran his hands through his hair for a few seconds, trying to get it to pick a direction and settle down. (He did not succeed. He never did.) Then he joined Lance in the hallway, and they walked downstairs together to the dining room.

His father sat at the head of the table, his black plaid uniform perfectly pressed, his black plaid crown exactly level above his thick blond eyebrows. He wore his rectangular, opaque silver glasses, as usual, so it was impossible to see his eyes. His mouth, barely visible under his moustache, was set in a firm line, but that was how it always looked. There was no way to tell whether it meant anything right now.

"Good morning, Father," Frederick ventured.

"Ah, good morning, boys."

He didn't *sound* like he was about to kill his youngest son. Maybe Lance had just been messing with him. Maybe Father wasn't even angry at Frederick in particular. He was pretty much always angry, just in general. Maybe this would just be a normal morning after all. Frederick slid into his seat at the table, feeling tentatively hopeful.

Lance pulled out his own chair, but Father stopped him.

"Not so fast, Lance. You know the rules. Last person seated has to do thirty push-ups."

"What? But that's only because when I came in earlier, you told me to go upstairs and get Frederick!"

The king shook his head. "Shouldn't have let your guard down, son. That's what fools do."

Lance sighed and dropped to the floor. "Yes, Dad." He started counting, wincing a little as he did so.

Blaine leaned toward him. "You okay there?"

"I've got a wicked sugar hangover," Lance said, not breaking his rhythm. "Totally worth it, though. Man, those waffles were good."

Father cleared his throat, and the boys fell silent. Mom was already silent; she never talked much at mealtimes. She preferred the company of her gourmet dessert magazines.

"My sons," the king said, "I uphold these rules because they train you for the harsh realities of life. Harsh realities that even an old man can fall prey to. For instance, take your visit to the Pastel Kingdom yesterday. I couldn't wait to visit. I wanted to embrace my dearest old friend, the Pastel King, whom I miss very much. I wanted to be there as our children fell in love, as we set wedding dates in place, and as our kingdoms grew closer."

He picked up his coffee and took a long, slow sip. "But last-minute duties popped up, and as the ruler of our glorious land, I had to put aside my personal wants and desires to do what was best for our kingdom. But then, that's what anyone of royal status would do, right, boys?"

Frederick concentrated very hard on spreading grape jelly on his lightly toasted sesame bagel. He was afraid the conversation was about to take an unfortunate turn. *Stay calm*, he told himself. *It still might all be fine.*

"So imagine my surprise," Father went on, "when I sat down to breakfast this morning to ask my eldest and most-preferred son how the excursion went, and he told me all about how"—and now his pleasant, serene tone suddenly transformed into loud and angry—"*you screwed everything up, Frederick!*"

Frederick lost hold of his jelly knife and his bagel, both of which went tumbling onto the tablecloth.

Father gripped his coffee mug so hard that it split in two, spilling coffee everywhere. He seemed oblivious to the hot liquid splattering his hands. "You wasted months of planning, and now the Pastel King thinks I'm hesitant about uniting our kingdoms! I let my guard down, and you—my stupid, selfish worm of a son—made a fool out of me!"

*Oh god*, Frederick thought, staring at his bagel. *I have to do this. I have to stand up to Father, just this once.* He forced himself to meet his father's eyes.

"Um, w-with all due respect, Father." He steeled himself, then rose to his feet. "I refuse to marry Gwendolyn!" When his father didn't immediately continue screaming at him, Frederick rushed on. "I do care about strengthening our alliance with the Pastel Kingdom. But Blaine and Lance are happy to go through with their engagements, which means the kingdoms will be successfully merged! So, frankly, it doesn't matter if I marry Gwendolyn or not."

He sat down again. No one said a word. His brothers looked shocked. Probably because Frederick had never dared to stand up to his father before. *You did it*, Frederick told himself. He couldn't quite manage to risk a glance at Father, so instead he picked up his bagel, trying to act nonchalant. *Now just stand your ground and conceal your fear. Father will have no choice but to back down.* He lifted the bagel to his mouth.

With a *whoosh*, the bagel was torn out of his grip just before he took a bite. Something had whipped past his face, so close he could feel it rushing by. Slowly, he turned his head. The bagel was . . . on the wall. Pinned there by Father's bread knife. It had been the knife that had zoomed right past his lips just then. Like . . . just past them. Almost touching. Feeling like he was moving in slow motion, he turned back to look at his father.

"Did you say it 'doesn't matter' if you marry Gwendolyn?" the king asked softly. "Do you have anything inside that permanently cowlicked, vomit-colored head of yours? Anyone who knows anything about the pure and unbreakable bond of sisterhood can foresee that if even one of those sisters is rejected by our family, all the sisters will refuse their marriage engagements out of solidarity."

In a flash the king lunged from his chair and grabbed Frederick by the collar. He sneered into his son's face. "So if you can't understand that your lack of affection toward one sister does affect all sisters, *does* affect our entire alliance with the Pastel Kingdom, and therefore *does* affect our kingdom's prosperity"—he gripped Frederick's chin with one hand and forcibly turned his head to look at the wall—"then you'll be trading places with that bagel."

"Dad—" Blaine started to interject, but the king waved him back to silence.

"So, Frederick," Father continued, "here is what is going to happen. You're all going back to the Pastel Kingdom again this weekend. And this time, you're going to show Princess Gwendolyn just how devoted you are. And I'm canceling all my plans so I can come along and make sure of it."

The king released his grip, and Frederick fell back into his seat. He kept his eyes on his now-empty plate, blinking back angry, hopeless tears. Of course he could never truly stand up to Father. None of them could, but him least of all. He would have to do what Father wanted, as always. And as always, what Frederick wanted wouldn't matter at all. Even if it involved his entire future and happiness.

Mother still hadn't said a word. Frederick knew she'd have her own eyes fixed on her magazine, pretending she couldn't hear the king screaming at her son. She never stood up to Father either. For just a moment, when father was threatening him, it had seemed like Blaine was going to try to intervene, and Frederick had felt a flare of hope that his brother cared enough about him even after their fight to try to help . . . but of course Blaine had backed down almost at once.

"Butler!" the king snapped, and the smartly dressed attendant stepped forward immediately. "Send a message to the Pastel Kingdom, urgently requesting their hospitality again this weekend. And make arrangements for three people to ride in the family carriage."

"Three?" Lance asked. "Won't you be riding in the carriage with us, Father?"

"Oh, I will be," the king agreed. "But Frederick won't. In order to give him some quality time to think about how to properly treat a lady, he's going to take Laverne there instead."

Blaine snickered—so much for thinking Blaine might have been on his side—and Lance laughed outright. Frederick just stared at his father in disbelief. Laverne was the king's pet llama. She was ridiculously spoiled and pampered and not exactly the kind of animal one would ride to an important meeting with a neighboring kingdom. Everyone at the Pastel Palace would be laughing at him if he showed up on the llama's back.

"You're going to make me ride Laverne?" he asked.

The king barked a mean laugh. "No, no—I wouldn't torture poor Laverne that way. No, you'll be hitched up to her traveling wagon, pulling her there in style. I think the princesses would enjoy meeting our sweet Laverne, don't you? And you can't expect her to walk all that way on her delicate little feet."

He couldn't be serious. He sounded serious, but he couldn't really expect— "Um, I can't tell if you're kidding, Father."

His father's cruel smile vanished. "I am not kidding, Frederick. You need to toughen up and learn to do what must be done for the good of the realm. And there needs to be some kind of punishment for your abysmal behavior at the Pastel Palace last night. You will be hitched up to Laverne's wagon like a pack animal and reflect during your long walk on how you can improve yourself and demonstrate to me that you're fit to be a prince of the Plaid Kingdom."

With that, his father rose and left the room. Lance had stopped laughing and was looking at Frederick with something like pity in his eyes. Blaine wasn't looking at Frederick, but he wasn't smirking anymore either.

"Maybe he'll change his mind before the weekend," Lance said finally. "Don't sweat it yet, li'l bro."

"Yeah," Frederick said. "Maybe."

But deep down, he couldn't quite make himself believe it.

# CHAPTER 10

## GWENDOLYN

"This is simply unacceptable!"

Miss Agatha glared around the royal classroom. Her face was even sterner than usual, her lavender eyes sparking over the rims of her half-moon glasses. Even her dark-violet hair looked irritated, the swirl of her customary bun seeming to coil even more tightly into itself, the tendrils that usually hung down to soften her slightly wrinkled face somehow conveying rigid disapproval. Gwen looked down at her desk, her stomach heavy with dread. She'd never forgotten to do her homework before. What was wrong with her? But of course she knew. With everything that had happened—the engagement news, the witch, meeting the princes, Jamie's wake, and . . . and the rest—school had just completely slipped her mind. She wasn't the only one, but somehow that didn't make her feel any better.

"I know you children all had an exciting weekend," Miss Agatha continued. "But royalty is about more than just fancy parties and handsome suitors! It is my duty to ensure that you also develop strong, creative, and disciplined minds that can guide and inspire the people around you." She stepped slowly around the room, smacking her long, white pointer into her palm to emphasize her words. "Today you were each supposed to hand in essays about what your extracurricular study will be for the year. But none of you wrote anything! I've never been so frustrated with you before."

Jamie raised his hand. "Miss Agatha? I didn't do my homework because I was poisoned."

Miss Agatha sighed and removed her glasses so that she could massage her temple. "Yes, I know, Jamie. You are excused, obviously."

"Miss Agatha?" Lorena asked. "Why do I feel so funny these past couple of days?"

"Miss Agatha?" Maria asked. "What is love?"

Miss Agatha put her glasses back on. "Well, I . . . I don't have the experience to—I mean, never mind that! Love is fleeting; only knowledge is forever. It's time to focus on your schooling! Since no one did their homework, let's have everyone state their extracurricular study plans in person right now."

Gwen sank lower into her seat. She hadn't even thought about her extracurricular study project. She'd originally been planning to brainstorm over the weekend and then decide on a focus and write up a tidy little essay for Miss Agatha, maybe with some pretty charts or graphs or something. But then Papa had made his announcement, and then . . .

"Jamie, let's start with you. As we all know, your career as a food critic has been prospering splendidly. I take it you'll continue to expand your clientele this year?"

"Yes, ma'am," Jamie said, flashing Miss Agatha a victory sign.

"Wonderful. You can write up your full proposal for me for next week." She turned to Maria. "And you, Maria? Will you continue your vocal performance studies this year?"

"Yes, Miss Agatha. I would like to hold a recital next spring."

"Very nice," Miss Agatha said, making a note on her clipboard. "Now, Lorena. Last year you surprised us with your, uh, intense one-woman rendition of Sun Wu's *The Beauty of War*. What, pray tell, will you grace us with this year?"

"Glad you asked!" Lorena said. "I was thinking of keeping the focus on defense this year. And I've got big plans, so I'll just tell you everything, starting from the top—"

"That's all right, Lorena," Miss Agatha interjected hastily. "I'll just wait for your essay. And make it one page or less this time, please."

Lorena gave their teacher an enthusiastic thumbs-up. "Roger that, Miss Agatha."

"And finally," Miss Agatha said, "we have Gwendolyn. What will your extracurricular focus be, dear?"

Gwen wanted to sink into the floor. What could she say? Miss Agatha was going to be so disappointed in her. She twisted the dark-green ribbons of her dress nervously.

"Um, I'm sorry, Miss Agatha, but—"

One of the windows suddenly imploded with an ear-splitting crash. Everyone screamed in surprise and alarm as a crow landed on Gwen's desk in a shower of broken glass. It held a piece of paper in its beak.

"Oh, the poor little crow!" Gwen was horrified, but thankfully the bird seemed only dazed, not dead. Then she took a closer look. *Wait a second.* "Psst!" she whispered. "Monika? Is that you?"

The crow nodded. Gwen leaned closer.

"Why did you crash through the window? Do you still need your glasses when you're a bird?"

The crow nodded again.

"Um, Gwennie," Maria said. "Are you *talking* to the strange bird that just crashed through the window and landed on your desk?"

"Oh, no, I—I was—"

"What is this?" Miss Agatha asked, snatching the paper that crow-Monika had been carrying. "A letter?" She ripped it open and began to read. "With great joy, we formally invite Princess Gwendolyn of the Pastel Kingdom to become a member of the . . . CPC."

Miss Agatha looked up from the letter, her face slack with what seemed to be shock.

*Oh no,* Gwen thought. *Oh no. That's the invitation to join the Cursed Princess Club!* She didn't know what to do. She'd promised not to tell anyone! She locked eyes with the agonized crow. They were both in so much trouble!

"My god, Gwendolyn," Miss Agatha said.

"I—" Gwen began, no idea what she was going to say.

"You brilliant girl!" Miss Agatha was positively beaming.

"Wha—?" Gwen began again.

"You were accepted into the CPC? The Cosmopolitan Princess Conservatory? That's the utmost renowned institution, exclusively open to only the most refined and elite princesses!" She fanned herself with the letter as she paced across the room. "This is the most ambitious extracurricular study I've ever heard of! I didn't even know they had a branch near our neck of the woods. But then they're very hush-hush, of course. Regardless, they are clearly acknowledging your formidable baking skills and numerous other talents!"

She turned to face the others. "Now, see, children? *This* is how you lay the groundwork for a successful future! Everyone, be more like Gwendolyn!"

"Gwennie, you're amazing!" Jamie said.

"Duh," Lorena added. "Gwen's the best!"

Gwen managed a shaky smile. She didn't trust herself to speak.

Miss Agatha whipped out her pencil and brushed the bits of glass from Gwen's desk onto the floor. "I'll just confirm that you'll be attending their initiation ceremony this Friday at twilight, and we'll send this back to their admissions office posthaste." She checked the box for yes on the letter, then stuffed it back in its envelope and shoved it into crow-Monika's beak. Then she tossed the bird back out through the hole in the broken window. "There we go."

Gwen gasped as Monika plummeted out of sight, but then, thank goodness, the crow-girl rose up again, flapping steadily. She dipped one wing at Gwen in an awkward bird-wave and then flew off toward the forest.

"Now, students," Miss Agatha said, "let's piggyback on this inspiring news and have you begin your essays now. After all, nothing strengthens one's intentions better than putting pen to paper."

"Yes, Miss Agatha," Gwen said along with her siblings. She picked up her pen. What was she going to write? She knew about the Cosmopolitan Princess Conservatory, of course—everyone did—but obviously they hadn't actually contacted her. She didn't know anything about what a real invitation from them would mean, or how she would have applied for one, or if they even accepted applications in that way? She'd never really considered looking into it, since she and the others had always had their own school with Miss Agatha. Why would she leave her family to attend school far away with strangers? She didn't care about being seen as "elite" or whatever.

Everyone else was already scribbling away—Maria with her pretty, loopy letters; Jamie with his neat, precise printing; Lorena with . . . well, so far it looked like she had mostly sketched out a bunch of battle formations without much text. Gwen didn't want to draw attention by being the only one not writing. She slowly penned *Cosmopolitan Princess Conservatory* at the top of her paper in careful, flowing script.

Suddenly the door flew open and Papa burst in. Everyone screamed again, but at least this time there wasn't any broken glass.

"Hey, kids! Guess what?" He held up a square piece of paper with a black-and-white plaid design. "I just heard from the Plaid king! He and the boys are all coming to visit us again this Saturday! How exciting is that!"

Maria and Lorena shrieked and jumped up and down, clutching each other.

Jamie joined them. "I finally get to meet the Plaid princes!"

Gwen felt frozen, unable to react. *They were coming back? Already?* Luckily no one seemed to notice her distress with all the cheering and shouting going on. She tried to look like she wasn't about to die inside.

The king started jumping up and down with the others. "Who cares about studying at a time like this, am I right?"

"Let's get ice cream!" Jamie shouted.

"Yeah!" Maria and Lorena agreed.

They all ran out the door. After an apologetic glance at Miss

Agatha, who clearly did not appreciate the unplanned early dismissal, Gwen walked slowly after the others. It was only Monday, she reminded herself. There was still time to—to prepare herself. In the meantime, maybe a giant scoop of ice cream would help. Jamie called back to her to hurry up, and she smiled, just a little. It certainly couldn't hurt, anyway.

~

The week seemed to fly by. Papa's interruption of class on Monday had given Gwen time to do a little research on the Cosmopolitan Princess Conservatory and write a reasonable-sounding essay for Miss Agatha. She felt terrible that she was lying to everyone, but what choice did she have? She also didn't seem to have a choice about joining the Cursed Princess Club. She hadn't felt like she belonged there, no matter what they thought. She had been planning to find a way to return Jolie's nightgown and thank them all again and then that would be the end of it. But there was no way to refuse now. If she did, Papa and Miss Agatha would demand to know why she didn't want to go to the Cosmopolitan Princess Conservatory. They might even contact the school, and then they'd find out it had all been a lie. Gwen would have to expose the truth about the Cursed Princess Club, and she couldn't allow that to happen.

And now it was Friday. Everyone else had spent the week

preparing for the princes' next visit tomorrow, but Gwen had made excuses to be busy with other things as much as possible. All day today she'd been so anxious that all she could do was bake endless batches of cookies. And now she had to head out, or she would never make it to the secret meeting location by twilight.

She packed up trays of cookies for all the staff and then made another tray to bring down to her family. They were in the living room for their weekly game night. Sounds of their good-natured teasing and laughing rose to meet her as she descended the stairs, and she felt a twinge of sadness that she had to miss out on the fun. She'd much prefer to stay here and play games than wander alone into the haunted forest and face the cursed princesses again. But then her sisters would probably just want to talk about the princes all night anyway. It was probably best for her to be somewhere else.

Gwen reached the first floor and stopped for a moment, taking in the scene before her. Lorena had just rolled the dice and was moving her token along the pink squares of the game board. They were playing Pretty Pretty Princess, and judging by the amount of costume jewelry Jamie was wearing compared to everyone else, he was definitely winning. Papa looked very funny in his bright-green beaded necklace, pink earrings, and yellow tiara. Maria must have picked the game; Gwen knew she loved this one. It was all about finding true love and acquiring lots of shiny accessories.

She made herself walk toward them. "Hi, everyone. I'm sorry I'm missing game night to attend the CPC initiation," she said, keeping her voice light. "Here are some cookies fresh from the oven to help make up for leaving!"

"Oh, Gwen, there's nothing to make up for!" Maria said. "We're so excited for you!"

"We totally are," said Lorena. "But also, yay for cookies!"

Jamie nodded enthusiastically, already reaching for the tray.

"Do you need a carriage drawn up or anything?" Maria asked.

"Um, no, that's okay. There are arrangements for me, behind the castle."

Maria shook her head. "Of course, what was I thinking? Obviously the CPC would take care of your transportation."

"Yes," Papa said. "I'm sure they've thought of everything. I'm not hip to all these fancy schools, but Miss Agatha tells me the Cosmopolitan Princess Conservatory is the best one, and I support them if they recognize the brilliance of our little Gwen!" Then he winked. "But mostly I support it because it doesn't sound co-ed."

Gwen tried not to think of Saffron; she couldn't risk her father sensing the existence of a boy in her evening plans.

"Well, I'd better get going!" she said, backing toward the door. "I love you! Don't wait up!"

"Have a great time, sweetie!" Papa said. "Love you!"

Gwen waved and fled, feeling the weight of all the lies piling up on top of her. *It will be okay*, she told herself. *The lies are only to protect the cursed princesses from discovery. Their need for secrecy is more important than my personal discomfort.* But then, she was also lying to her sisters about Frederick. That was also for their own protection, though. She couldn't let them find out the truth and ruin their own happiness. Lying had to be okay if you did it to protect the people you loved.

Gwen snuck out the side entrance and ran toward the forest.

# CHAPTER 11

## GWENDOLYN

The trees seemed to crowd tightly together as soon as she stepped onto the path. Silence and darkness descended upon her even though the sun was still setting, painting the western sky with pink and purple and gold.

*There's nothing to be afraid of,* Gwen told herself, hugging her arms around her chest against the sudden chill. Sure, it was called the haunted forest, but that was just a *name*, it wasn't like it really meant anything. Surely the princesses wouldn't have a headquarters in the middle of the forest if it was truly dangerous! Right? Anyway, she had already been through the forest twice already. It was certainly *spooky* in the dark, but it was perfectly safe. Probably perfectly safe. And if anything jumped out and grabbed her and dragged her away screaming . . . well, maybe Princess Calpernia and the others would come looking for her. Maybe they'd even find her before it was too late.

*Stop it.* She kept walking, trying not to peer too closely into any of the shadows between the trees. Especially the ones that seemed like they might be moving. It wasn't too far—she just had to keep her eyes on the path and move forward. One step after another. The bits of sky she could still see deepened from purple to black.

"Hello, Gwendolyn," a voice said from the darkness ahead.

For a moment Gwen felt the echo of her terror from her last nighttime run into the forest, but she fought it down. She knew that voice.

"Hello, Princess Calpernia."

The blue-haired woman stepped forward into a shaft of moonlight. Saffron stood on her right, his goblin hand hidden in a long, leather glove. Jolie stood on her left, the gaping holes of her eyes unmasked and glowing with an unnatural light. All three wore long, brown cloaks. "Welcome," Calpernia said, "to your initiation to the Cursed Princess Club."

Gwen swallowed nervously. Somehow she hadn't expected it to be this . . . ominous.

But then Calpernia smiled, and the mood lifted at once. "We're really glad you decided to join the club! I honestly didn't think you would."

"I didn't think I would either," Gwen admitted.

Calpernia crossed her arms. "Before we can declare you an official member, though, we have some prerequisites for you to complete."

"Like what?" Gwen hated how quickly she jumped to being on her guard again, but really, the choice of location was not helping! It was hard to feel open-minded and trusting in the middle of the scary forest.

"First, you must vow to obey the five sacred commandments of the Cursed Princess Club. And to help you remember these commandments, we have a little keepsake for you." She turned slightly. "Jolie, if you would?"

Jolie rummaged around under her cloak and pulled out a small fluffy ball on a thin pink loop of cord. She held it up, and Gwen saw that the ball had a cute panda face with long eyelashes and a tiny crown. Its little pink tongue was sticking out playfully.

"Our commandments follow a simple acronym, which is P.A.N.D.A." Jolie explained. "So if you ever forget, you can just remember Princess Panda! I'll clip her to your backpack for you."

"Panda?" Gwen repeated, confused.

Princess Calpernia nodded. "The *P* stands for 'Prince Charming is not necessary for a happily ever after!'"

"The first *A* is for 'Assist others'!" Jolie said next. "We try our best to help each other and the community when we can."

Saffron leaned forward. "*N* means 'Never tell anyone about the Cursed Princess Club, ever.'"

Gwen started to relax. Honestly, this was all very wholesome so far.

"*D*," said Calpernia, "stands for 'Don't go near the barn.'" Her smile vanished, and she looked at Gwen very seriously, her golden eyes hard and flat and deadly. A small animal cried mournfully somewhere in the darkness. "The final *A* stands for 'Again, don't go anywhere near the barn.'"

"What's in the barn?" Gwen asked softly.

Calpernia's smile flashed back into existence, and her eyes lost that terrifying dead quality. "Don't worry about it, kiddo. So! What do you think? Do you vow to adhere to the club's rules?"

*Well, I guess I wasn't planning on going into any barns anyway.* Gwen nodded. "Okay. I vow to obey the five commandments of the Cursed Princess Club."

"Wonderful!" said Calpernia. "Then we'll move to the last little step—the all-night trial!"

"The what?!"

"It's a test that some consider grueling, ear shattering, extremely invasive, and mortifying," Calpernia said. "But it's a wonderful tool for measuring one's character and perseverance." Her smile was growing wider by the second. "And if your body remains after dawn, the other members will be the final judges as to whether you pass or not."

Gwen had been right the first time. These people were terrifying. She had to get out of here. *I'll just back away, and I'll go home and tell everyone it was a big misunderstanding. This is what I get for lying to my family.* But before she could move, Saffron and Jolie each grabbed one of her arms and began to drag her toward a large tent beyond the next set of trees. Hushed whispers came from within, and she shuddered to think of what might be waiting for her inside.

"Here we go!" Calpernia said, her smile enormous now, stretching the sides of her attractive face. "Good luck, Gwendolyn. It's time for a—"

"No!" Gwen cried, trying to wrench free. "Stop! I didn't agree to this!"

The curtains flew dramatically open.

"SLUMBER PARTY!" everyone yelled.

Gwen only barely managed to keep herself from screaming before the words registered. What? Seriously, just—what?

The other Cursed Princess Club members were all there, lounging on blankets in their pajamas. Piles of snacks and games and magazines and beauty supplies were scattered around them. Strings of party lights had been turned on when the curtains opened, and an assortment of pretty paper lanterns hung from the tent support poles, giving the entire scene a festive, cheery glow.

"Huh?" Gwen finally managed, weakly.

Jolie took her arm—far more gently than a few moments before—and led her into the tent. "Sorry about scaring you," she said. "It's kind of a tradition. But wasn't it fun to find out it wasn't something horrible after all?"

Gwen didn't say anything. She wasn't entirely certain yet that this wasn't still something horrible. Her breathing hadn't quite returned to normal, and her head was reeling from the psychological roller coaster of the last few minutes. She also hadn't been prepared—emotionally or, like, with toiletries—to spend a whole night with these people, who really were still total strangers. She did, at least, have Jolie's freshly washed nightgown, which she'd brought with her to return.

The girls showed her where she could get undressed. Gwen stood alone in the makeshift changing room, wondering for a few final seconds whether she should still try to run home and declare all of this a terrible mistake. Then she got Jolie's nightgown out of her bag and changed into it. She had to stay; it would be inexcusably rude to refuse their hospitality, especially after they'd apparently gone to so much trouble to set up this party.

But on top of that, she realized she didn't want to leave. Yes, some of these girls were a bit . . . startling, but so far they'd all been nothing but nice to her. (Except for the scaring bit, but now that that part was over, she wasn't really too mad about it.) They *had* hurt her feelings with all the curse stuff, but then, if all of them were cursed themselves, she supposed she could understand why they would have jumped to conclusions. Even though it was still painful to think about how quickly they'd assumed her appearance was a curse. But she owed them the chance to get to know them.

And maybe she owed herself the chance too. To let them get to know her.

When Gwen emerged, Monika ran over and hugged her. "I'm so glad you came!" She glanced around, then added in a whisper, "I'm also really glad everything worked out okay and we didn't get in trouble!"

"Me too," Gwen agreed. She let Monika lead her over to one of the blankets where Abbi was waving them to sit down. "So that was all made up, what Princess Cal—"

"Oh, you have to call her Prez, now that you're one of us!" Monika interrupted.

"Um, okay, what Prez said about a grueling, mortifying, character-measuring ordeal?" She was pretty sure the scare-the-new-girl part was over, but it seemed wise just to confirm.

"Ha," Abbi said. "Those were all actual complaints, mostly from Saffron. He really hates slumber parties."

Without preamble, she and Monika settled onto either side of Gwen and began to play with her hair, sweeping it up into two high ponytails like it was the most natural thing in the world. Maybe it was; Gwen had no experience with any of this, after all. And their gentle fingers moving through her hair felt kind of nice.

"But slumber parties really are a great test of one's character," Monika said. "You can learn a lot about someone through all the laughter, stupid games, and lack of sleep."

"Really?" Gwen asked. They were doing something more elaborate to her hair now, twisting it up and around itself somehow. There also seemed to be a great many tiny pink bows and bobby pins involved.

"Take Prez and Saffron, for instance." Monika nodded toward the other side of the tent, where the two people in question were now locked in a ferocious game of Ping-Pong. "They gravitated right to the Ping-Pong table, showing that they have strong athletic and competitive proclivities."

"If I beat you," Saffron called to Prez, "I get to be the new president of the Cursed Princess Club, and I'm changing the name!"

"It's funny," Prez said back. "You say the same thing every time we play, and yet you've never beaten me. I take it as a sign that you're actually quite fond of the name!"

Saffron growled and served for the next point.

Monika continued, "The power dynamics between people really become clear."

"Dang it," Abbi said abruptly. "I just need one more bobby pin to finish Gwen's hair. Jolie, you got a spare?"

Jolie had put her eye mask on at some point since they'd arrived, but now she lifted it so she could reach inside her eye hole. Gwen tried not to shiver with revulsion. Jolie was so sweet, but her curse was so creepy!

She pulled out a silver bobby pin. "Here you go, Abbi."

"Thanks, boo."

Monika's eyes suddenly went wide and intense. "Ooh, that's pretty and shiny! Can I have it?"

"No!" Abbi said, swatting Monika's hand away. "This is for Gwen."

An agonized groan from the Ping-Pong table made them all turn to look. Saffron's goblin hand was wrapped around his other wrist, pulling the paddle from where Saffron wanted it to be. "No!" he said, struggling to pull it back. "Come on, quit it! I'm just about to w—"

With a *thwack*, the ball bounced off the paddle at a crazy angle. It flew across the tent and landed squarely inside Jolie's left eye hole. Gwen gasped, but Jolie was laughing, so apparently it hadn't hurt or lodged itself in her brain or anything. Gwen still wasn't sure exactly how things worked in there.

Monika leaned over and said, "Slumber parties are also a great way to observe how people deal with problems and confrontation."

With a sigh, Saffron approached Jolie. "Um, I'm really sorry, but I think we dropped something in your . . . skull."

"That's okay, Saffron!" Jolie said easily.

"Thanks. You're always so sweet—"

"But you'll have to get it out yourself."

Saffron's face went a little green, but he seemed unwilling to admit defeat. ". . . 'Kay. Sure. No prob."

They all watched as he screwed up his face and reached inside Jolie's eye socket. Jolie was laughing even harder now.

"Wow," Gwen said. "You're right, Monika. This is super informative." She'd only ever had slumber parties with her own family, so the learning opportunities weren't really the same. "If it's not impolite, I'd also love to hear more about everyone's curses, though. We didn't finish talking about them last time."

"Ooh, learn about me!" someone said. Gwen turned to see the woman who'd offered her wine that first morning. But this time she had a new feature: a pointy nose that had to be a good five inches long. "Remember me from your last visit? My name's Princess Syrah of the Metallic Kingdom! Would you like some champagne?"

"Um, no, no champagne," Gwen said. "I'm still sixteen. But yes, I do remember you! Although I feel like you, um, look a little different?"

"Oh, yeah, ha-ha. You mean this, right?" She pointed to her nose. "I must have been having a good nose day when we met. A few years ago, a jealous boyfriend suspected me of cheating on him. So he gave me chocolates infused with the typical Pinocchio's Nose Curse to find out if I was lying to him. And since then, every time I tell a lie, my nose grows in proportion to the severity of the untruthfulness. But it always eventually returns to its normal size."

"Wow," Gwen said, feeling sorry for her. "Did he feel terrible about what he did, after?"

"Um, no, because he was right. I was totally cheating on him. So I think he felt pretty good about the whole thing."

"Oh," Gwen said.

Syrah shrugged. "It's okay, really. Unlike most of the girls here, I don't let my curse hold me back from having a fun time with gentlemen suitors. So if you ever need relationship advice or anything, I'm your girl!" She tilted her head and got a sudden gleam in her eye. "*Do* you have any gentlemen suitors or Prince Charmings in your life?"

"Oh," Gwen said again. "Um, well . . . I mean, I guess?"

All the other girls immediately crowded around.

"Tell us everything," Syrah commanded.

"No, no—it's not—it's nothing, really. He's just an arranged fiancé, and, I mean . . ." She blinked rapidly, her eyes going blurry. *Am I tearing up? Oh no, not now. I don't want to cry in front of everyone!* She realized she was tugging at her hair nervously, pulling out all the little ribbons and pins Monika and Abbi had put in. "He doesn't—he doesn't even . . ." And then the tears spilled over, and she could only whisper the rest. ". . . want me."

And then Syrah was hugging her, which somehow made her sob even harder. "Gwen! Hey, it's okay. Just let it out."

So she did. She hadn't really let herself cry since that night.

She'd tried not to think about it at all, just pushing the memory deeper and deeper inside and doing everything she could to hide her feelings from her family. It was such a relief to just feel all the pain and sadness and stop trying to fight it.

And then, once the tears had run their course and she was down to just the occasional wet sniffle, she told the cursed princesses everything.

# CHAPTER 12

## GWENDOLYN

When Gwen finished, everyone was quiet for a moment. She'd told them the whole story, from her initial excitement at seeing Frederick's portrait, to the confusing awkwardness of that first tea meeting, to the awful words she'd overheard while recapturing Jamie's wayward waffle bunny. It had been terrible to relive it, but she couldn't deny that she felt a lot better now. Still sad, but lighter, for sharing her burden.

"Well," said Abbi, finally. "I think it's pretty clear that we should go punch this prince in the throat."

"No punching, Abbi," said Prez. "I've got a machete in the house. I can go now and—"

"No!" Gwen said, horrified. "No violence at all!"

They both stared at her.

"You can't just let this guy talk about you like that!" Prez said.

"Yeah," Abbi said. "He's a jerk who hurt your feelings. You need to give him what he deserves!"

"*I know, but I can't worry about that right now!*" Gwen shouted. She took a breath and got her voice back under control. "Sorry for yelling. But all I can handle right now is how to face Frederick and move forward without ruining the engagements for my sisters."

"You care about your sisters' happiness with the princes that much more than your own?" Jolie asked.

Gwen traced the shape of a heart on the blanket with her toe. "You'd understand if you saw how in love they are. And the other princes are really great. I think they'd be wonderful matches for my sisters, both of them. I can't ruin all of that just because . . . " She didn't finish, but she didn't need to. They all knew now.

Prez shook her head. "You're considerate, kiddo, I'll give you that. Too considerate, if you ask me. But it's your decision. But I still think that you should confront him about what he said and give him an earful about how a gentleman should properly speak about young ladies. It will also give you some closure."

"Confront him? I can't do that!" Gwen said.

"Hmm," Syrah said, pushing up from the blanket and getting to her feet. "I agree with Prez. Talking to him is the right thing to do. But it doesn't have to be confrontational, just honest.

Here—why don't I role-play what I would say to Frederick if I were you. Abbi, come here. You pretend to be Frederick, okay?"

Abbi got up to stand beside Syrah. "Uh, okay. Hey, Gwen, what's this loser Frederick look like, anyway?"

"He has big, pretty, green eyes and blond hair that kind of goes like this, and also like this." She tried to re-create the unruly tendencies of Frederick's hair, spreading her fingers and moving them up and down on opposite sides of her head in slightly different directions. Abbi made squinty eyes at her.

"Okay," Syrah said, "so I'm Gwen, and this is what I'd say once I ran into Frederick." She cleared her throat. "Hey, Frederick. Can we talk for a second?"

"Ugh, I'm busy doing my hair, which Gwen makes sound like a broom that dried at a weird angle," Abbi said in a voice that she was clearly trying to make sound deeper and kind of dopey. "But whatever, talk if you want."

Syrah sighed but kept going. "Okay, thanks. I want you to know that I overheard what you said about me the other night. It hurt my feelings, but I understand."

"Busted," Abbi said in her fake-Frederick voice.

"I'm fine not being your fiancé, and I will gladly stand on the sidelines as your friend and sister-in-law. I just want you and everyone in our families to be happy."

"Bruh," Abbi said, putting a hand to her heart. "That's so big of you, especially when I've been such a butt."

Gwen giggled. Frederick didn't talk anything like that, of course, but Abbi's rendition was pretty funny.

"So something like that!" Syrah said. "It takes the pressure off both of you to force a romantic relationship. And he'll be stunned that you're so mature and confident."

Gwen was surprised to find that she liked Syrah's idea a lot. "That was really helpful! And what you said was perfect—I'll try to say it to him just like that, word for word. Thank you so much!"

Syrah winked at her. "My pleasure, babe."

"And who knows!" Monika put in. "Prince Frederick could start to fall for Gwen the instant she walks away! Boys are like that sometimes, right, Syrah?"

"Um, sure," Syrah said. Her nose instantly gained another inch.

"Hey!" said Monika. "You don't think that at all! You were lying!"

"Well, you backed me into a corner! How's a girl supposed to respond to that?"

"Please," said a new voice. It was the part-lobster princess, who was reclining on a big pile of pillows. "You know there is only one way to find out what will happen in the future when it comes to men." She held up a folded paper contraption in one giant claw. "You must consult the fortune teller!"

"Ooh, nice, Thermidora," Monika said. "That's a staple of any successful slumber party!"

"Your name is Princess Thermidora?" Gwen asked.

"Yes! Good evening, Gwendolyn. I hope you're enjoying our soirée."

"I am, thank you!" She hesitated, then went on, "Um, Thermidora? Would it be rude of me to ask what kind of curse turned you into part lobster?"

Thermidora drew herself up and narrowed her eyes. "Why, yes! That is very rude!"

"I'm so sorry! I shouldn't have pried!"

Thermidora shook her head impatiently. "It is rude of you to assume I was cursed *into* a lobster, when it's quite the opposite!" She raised one red pincer to her forehead dramatically. "I am a luscious lobster princess who has been cursed into this hideous human body! A devious sea cucumber was jealous of my perfect relationship with Benedict, the most handsome lobster baron. She cast a spell to turn me human, so that I'd have to abandon my kingdom and the ocean altogether, choking for air. Then she could keep my Benedict all to herself. But thank goodness, she's an inept slug, and her spell left my immaculate pincers intact. Eventually Prez found me and kindly brought me to the Cursed Princess Club. I love this new family, but I still sit in my room every night, longing to return to the sea in my true form."

Gwen put a hand gently on Thermidora's shoulder. "I'm so sorry. It must be terrible to be torn from your home that way."

"You're a kind girl," Thermidora said, apparently forgiving

Gwen's earlier rudeness. Gwen made a mental note to try not to make assumptions about anyone's curses from now on. "Now!" the lobster princess continued. "It is time for fortune telling! Saffron, you're going first. Pick a color."

Saffron tried to beg off, but Thermidora raised a shiny red pincer at him menacingly. "Okay, okay! I pick purple!"

"Wonderful," she said. She placed the tips of her pincers inside the paper contraption and moved it, opening and closing the center first one way and then another, several times. Then she lifted one corner of folded paper. "The fortune teller predicts that . . . you will marry a whale prince, live in a toilet, and give birth to eighty-nine sea urchins."

Everyone laughed, and Saffron just sat down grumpily. "Well, I'm *pretty* sure I won't do any of that."

"You're next, Syrah!" Thermidora said.

"Okay! I pick pink!"

Thermidora repeated the process with her paper-thing and lifted another corner. "You're going to live in a mansion made entirely of egg salad, and no one will ever kiss you again!"

"Nooooo!" Syrah seemed to have temporarily forgotten that it was just a game.

"Ooh, do Prez next!" Monika said.

"Sure, why not?" Prez said. "I pick blue."

"All right, let's see," said Thermidora. "Prez is going to marry a poor man, live in a one-bedroom house with a white picket fence, and have four children." The lobster princess frowned. "Well, that's not very funny. That's just prudent and slightly endearing."

"Hey!" Monika said. "Prez, doesn't that kinda sound like what you—" But then they all saw Prez's face, and Monika flushed bright red. "Oh my god! I'm so sorry! I don't know what I was thinking!"

Prez gave Monika a sad smile. "I—it's okay, Monika. I was actually just gonna get up and refill some snacks. Back in a minute." She walked out of the tent without looking back.

Gwen looked around at the others, confused. "What was that about? Is Prez okay?" But no one would meet her eye. Did it have something to do with Prez's curse? She still hadn't learned what that was. But the fortune had seemed so innocent . . .

Monika suddenly lunged at Thermidora and grabbed the paper fortune teller.

"Hey!" Thermidora shouted. "What are you doing?"

"I'm taking this away! It's making everyone feel awful!"

"Knock it off! I haven't told Gwen's fortune yet!" She picked up one of her pillows and smacked Monika in the face with it.

Monika fell to the floor. Saffron, Syrah, and Jolie all looked at one another and yelled, "Pillow fight!"

The tent erupted into chaos.

Pillows were flying everywhere, and everyone was shouting and laughing and running around. Monika turned into a crow after another pillow hit her, and she flew to Gwen's arms, cawing pitifully. Gwen caught her gently and backed into a corner, watching the rest of them go at it. It was kind of hilarious. At one point, everyone ganged up on Saffron, but his goblin hand seemed to be super excited about the pillow battle and was doing its best to help. It even blocked pillows that were coming from angles Saffron couldn't easily see. When he'd fought everyone off, he high-fived himself proudly. Gwen and crow-Monika looked at each other and laughed. Gwen was pretty sure Monika was laughing, anyway. Her caws now sounded mirthful rather than scared. She seemed to be feeling okay now that she was safely out of the action.

"*Hey!*" A girl Gwen had never seen before was standing in the entranceway, holding the tent flaps open so she could glare at them. She was very scary, with shaggy red hair and intense, angry eyes that had red sclerae and white pupils. She was dressed in black-and-white stripes with ripped sleeves and looked positively insane with rage. "*Why are you all screaming in the middle of the night?!*"

The pillow fight stopped at once, but no one else seemed alarmed. Except Monika, who rose up in a flurry of feathers and darted to the far side of the tent.

"Oh, hi, Nell!" Jolie said, skipping over to where Gwen was cowering. "This is Gwen, she's the newest member of—"

"*Do I look like I care?*" Nell shouted. "*Just keep it down. It's late!*"

"Okay, we will!" Jolie said. "Good night!"

Nell growled incoherently and stalked out, letting the tent flaps fall closed behind her.

"That was Princess Nell of the Striped Kingdom," Jolie said. "Don't mind her. She sort of does her own thing."

"She's right, though," Syrah said. "It's late. We should go to bed."

That sounded like a very good idea. Gwen was having way more fun than she'd ever expected, but she was also pretty beat. Several of the girls and Saffron ran around collecting the pillows from various corners and laid them out on the floor-blankets. Thermidora retrieved another pile of blankets from a corner and handed—clawed?—them out for everyone to snuggle under.

"Come sleep next to me!" Monika said to Gwen, grabbing her arm. She was back in her human form again, so she had hands and everything. "I got us a great blanket already."

Gwen let herself be towed to the spot Monika had picked out. She'd gotten Gwen a pillow too. Abbi and Syrah were setting up their own sleeping spots nearby. After a few last calls of good night from around the tent, everyone settled down and got quiet.

Gwen lay down on her back, savoring the plump softness of the pillow and the faint scent of lavender fabric softener. What a night this had been! She hadn't known what the initiation would involve, but she certainly hadn't expected this. All of the princesses had been so kind and welcoming, so ready to accept her as one of them. It was such a contrast to how Frederick had treated her that it almost made her start tearing up again. Knowing these people liked her and wanted her to be around . . . that they'd been so angry on her behalf and so ready to defend her . . . but also that they respected her wishes about no violence and helped her come up with a different solution . . . it all made her feel very safe in a way that she'd never felt with anyone other than her own family.

Monika was snoring softly beside her, still holding on to Gwen's arm. Gwen smiled, feeling suddenly very lucky that she'd run into the forest that night. Maybe sometimes even the worst things could lead to something good.

~

The next morning, after getting dressed and packing up their things, they all gathered for breakfast on the club's lovely patio. Prez poured everyone a glass of orange juice and then raised hers in a toast.

"Here's to Gwen, the newest official member of the Cursed Princess Club!" Everyone cheered and clinked their glasses. Gwen blushed, not used to being the center of attention, but she couldn't help smiling. Prez smiled back and said, "We're really happy you're part of our little group, kiddo."

Prez seemed fine this morning, betraying no trace of what had upset her last night. Gwen wasn't sure if she'd ever returned to the tent to go to sleep; by the time the rest of them blinked blearily awake, Prez had been back at the house. Gwen certainly wasn't going to bring up what was clearly a sensitive topic, but maybe she could ask one of the other girls later to explain what had happened. Just so she didn't inadvertently say something wrong in the future.

A tray of cinnamon buns appeared before them, and Gwen looked up to see a handsome man dressed in a black tailcoat with a blue vest and a blue tie adorned with a golden pentagon. The buns smelled amazing.

"Enjoy, madams," he said with a little bow.

"Ah, Gwen—this is my butler, Curtis. He takes care of the cooking and errands for the house."

"It is a pleasure to meet you, Miss Gwen."

"It's a pleasure to meet you, too, Curtis!" she said. "And these cinnamon buns look delicious!"

"Yeah, nice buns, Curtis!" Syrah said, snickering. Beside her, Monika and Abbi dissolved into badly concealed laughter.

Curtis fixed them with an unamused gaze. "I don't know what you ladies have scheduled in your planners for today, but I hope you have something loftier in mind than utilizing your extreme privilege to objectify the person who cooks and cleans for you."

The girls stopped laughing at once, looking ashamed. Prez shook her head and turned back to Gwen.

"So how often do you think you can stop by our club? Some of us are here every day, while other princesses only come by when they need support."

Gwen considered. "Well, since my family and teacher think

this is some sort of institute I'm studying at, I think I need to come a few afternoons every week."

"An institute, hm?" Prez said. "I do sometimes give lectures, and I think everyone here can attest that they're not only informative but also very engaging. Right, ladies?"

All the princesses suddenly became very interested in their cinnamon rolls.

"Please don't make me tell a lie, Prez," said Syrah, pointing to her nose, which had returned to its original size. "I want to keep this face for my date tonight."

"I do think we each have things we can teach you about being a sophisticated princess," said Thermidora.

"Like how to talk to uncivilized, jerky princes you happen to be engaged to," Syrah added with a wink.

"Oh, that's right!" Gwen said. She'd nearly forgotten! "Today's the day the Plaid princes are visiting again!"

"Do you feel ready to talk to Frederick now?" Syrah asked.

"Yes! I'm going to take your excellent advice and just have a nice, honest conversation with him." She looked around at the rest of the group. "Um, I also just want to thank everyone. I was feeling really lost about things lately, and you all comforted me and helped guide me in the right direction. I'm really grateful for your help."

"You're welcome!" Prez said. "Helping each other is what we strive to do here, after all!"

Gwen finished her last bite of cinnamon bun—they really

were delicious—and stood up. "I should get going. Oh, but Jolie, before I go, I wanted to return your nightgown. Thank you for lending it to me twice now!"

"I was happy to!" Jolie said. "Come to think of it, where is your green dress? I know I washed and hung it up the other day."

Monika gasped and then began chomping on her bun, avoiding eye contact.

Syrah stood up and pointed at her. "Monika! Did you steal Gwen's dress?"

Monika leapt from her chair and ran from the room, shouting, *"It's mine now and you can't have it back!"*

Gwen stared after her, too surprised to say anything. Monika had been so nice to her! Why—?

Prez sighed. "Gwen, did you know that crows love collecting shiny, pretty objects?"

*Ohhhhh.* It was a crow thing.

"She steals all our nice things and hoards them in her mess of a room!" Abbi explained grouchily.

Monika stuck her head out of an upper-floor window that looked out over the patio. "They make me feel happy and safe!" She held up Gwen's green dress. "Like this dress!"

"Monika! Give it back!" Syrah yelled up to her.

"*No!*"

"I—it's okay!" Gwen said hurriedly. "She can keep it! I made that dress, and it'll be easy to sew another one."

"Really?" Monika called down.

Gwen smiled up at her. "Yes, really. I want you to have it."

She hugged the dress to her tightly. "Yay! Thank you, Gwen!"

And with that it was really time for her to go. Gwen said her goodbyes and walked into the forest, which, again, was much less scary in the daylight. She was amazed to realize that she was actually looking forward to the princes' visit now. She'd never be able to thank Syrah and the others enough for their advice on how to resolve things with Frederick. She picked up her pace, all the while repeating Syrah's words in her head to make sure she remembered them exactly. She hoped she wouldn't get nervous and mess it up! But first things first: she had to get home and change. She wanted to be sure she was fully prepared for the princes' arrival, unlike last time.

Today was the day everything would get better.

# CHAPTER 13

## FREDERICK

Father had not changed his mind.

In the end, at least, he hadn't actually strapped Frederick into one of the horses' harnesses, but he did make him pull Laverne in her little cart all the way to the Pastel Kingdom. Not that Frederick had arrived yet. He thought there were just a few more miles left, though.

"You doing okay back there, Laverne?" he called over his shoulder. He was afraid if he stopped to check on her he wouldn't be able to muster the will to start moving again. She bleated in a put-upon way that he interpreted as annoyance with the bumpy ride but no actual distress. She was a very expressive bleater.

He'd had to wrestle her to get her into the cart, so now he

smelled like llama in addition to being sweaty and dirty from the hours of pulling the not-small creature along the rocky dirt road. He couldn't believe this was happening. He was going to arrive late and filthy and stinky and would still have to entertain a princess he had no intention of marrying once he got there. Why was he doing this? Oh, right. Because his life literally depended on it. He could still feel the knife brushing his lips as it speared the bagel from between his fingers. He didn't want to believe his father would *really* kill him, but the king got so angry sometimes . . . it seemed wisest not to risk disobeying him any further. At least for the time being.

Maybe this visit wouldn't be so bad. He was prepared now, anyway. He wouldn't have to endure the same shock and disappointment of finding out he'd been wrong about his intended bride. And really, he hadn't exactly given Gwendolyn much of a chance. He'd barely spoken with her at all, in fact. He felt a little twinge of guilt at that. It wasn't her fault there had been that enormous misunderstanding. It probably couldn't hurt to get to know her a little. Not that he could see ever being able to get past her appearance, but he could certainly at least be civil. He didn't really want to think about how his lack of interest might be making her feel. He'd been so caught up in his own misfortune, he hadn't really considered that she might have feelings at all. That . . . wasn't super great of him.

He shifted the cart handles under his arms and tried to pick up his pace. The sooner he got there, the better. At least the countryside was pretty. The road took them along the edge of a mountain, and although pulling Laverne up the steep incline had *not* been fun, the view was really something. To his left, craggy cliffs fell away to show great swaths of the Pastel landscape, including glimpses of the famous haunted forest. He turned his head to take in the blue sky, the rolling hills far below, and the scattered fields of sunflowers.

*Sunflowers.*

Without warning, his mind dragged him back to boarding school, to that first terrible night. He'd done his best to bury those memories deep, deep inside, but sometimes they escaped the tiny prison he'd created for them. He couldn't breathe. He was in the terrifying, close darkness of his locked trunk. He heard the other boys laughing. The horrible boys who had called him sunflower because of his stupid hair and tortured him because—

No. *No!* He wasn't going to relive that. Not again. Those days were over.

With a furious shout he shook himself free of the cart handles and let them fall to the ground. The cart tilted, and Laverne bleated angrily. He was done with this stupid punishment. Hadn't he already been punished enough?

"That's it," he told Laverne. "Out of the cart. You're going to carry *me* the rest of the way."

He yanked her out by her jeweled collar and climbed onto her fluffy back while she was still too surprised to resist. "Take me to the Pastel Palace! I command you!"

Slowly, she turned to look at him over her shoulder. Her expression was not one of agreeable compliance.

He suddenly had a very bad feeling. "Um, please?" he added in a small voice.

She bucked and flung him off so violently that he rolled several feet and tumbled over the small ledge at the side of the road. Then she trotted off without him.

He lay there for a few minutes, breathing hard. This trip could not get any worse.

Then he rolled over and saw the much larger cliff he'd come within inches of also tumbling off. *Oh. I guess it could have been a lot worse, actually.* The ground was very far away. It . . . would not have been a survivable distance to fall.

He scrambled away from the edge. Then he noticed small figures down in a grassy clearing in the forest far below. They were wearing gowns and tiaras and seemed to be doing some kind of odd coordinated dance? It was hard to tell from here, but if he squinted, one of them looked like she might be an old lady, and another seemed to have an extremely long nose. Faintly, he heard a girl's voice saying "And bend! And stretch!"

He shook his head. These backwater kingdoms always had such weirdos.

He got to his feet, careful to stay away from the drop-off. He tried dusting off his pants, but he was already so dirty it hardly made a difference at this point. He climbed back up to the road and started walking in the direction Laverne had gone.

And then stopped, staring.

A girl was sitting at the edge of the cliff up ahead, looking out at the view. He couldn't make out the color of her hair in the glare of the sunlight, but he'd recognize that abhorrent green and white dress with the orange bows anywhere. Didn't she have any other clothes?

"Gwendolyn? Hello?"

She didn't seem to hear him. With a defeated sigh, he started walking toward her. He might as well get this courtship over with as soon possible. He reached out to touch her shoulder. "Hey—"

She screamed in surprise and lurched away from him. And then, arms waving wildly, she fell off the cliff.

For a moment he was too stunned to move. Then he ran forward to the edge, desperately hoping to find her grasping a sturdy rock or tree root or something with both hands. He would pull her up, and—

But she was gone. He stared down, but all he saw was a low-flying crow darting off for the cover of the trees. She must have fallen all the way to the bottom. Which meant—which meant—

He collapsed to his knees, holding his head in his hands.

He had just murdered his fiancé.

~

Frederick wasn't sure how long he knelt at the edge of the cliff, wishing for time to go backward. At some point he must have gotten to his feet, must have started walking, because there was the Pastel Palace, looming prettily before him in the late afternoon light. Molly opened the front door as he approached and let him in without commenting on his lateness or his appearance. She led him down the same hallway that they'd gone through last time, the one that had led to his greatest disappointment. And now it would lead him to worse, surely, once he confessed to what he'd done.

He stumbled through the doorway, mumbling greetings and apologies, making his painful way across the room to where Blaine was openly staring at him. Everyone was staring, in fact. He must look a sight, but that didn't matter now. Did anything matter anymore?

"Blaine," he said, coming up behind the sofa where his brothers were sitting. He spoke softly, but the room was so quiet that everyone could hear him anyway. "Blaine, I need to talk to you. In—in private."

"Uh, sure, okay," Blaine said warily. "Why don't you go, uh, freshen up, because you look—and smell—awful, and I'll meet you in the hall in few minutes?"

"Oh. Okay. Sure." He turned to ask Maria where the bathroom was, but before he could open his mouth she just pointed wordlessly to another door. Her eyes were wide as he nodded his thanks and headed out into another hallway. He stepped along the light-blue carpet, barely seeing where he was going. This couldn't be happening. It couldn't. If only he hadn't startled Gwendolyn that way. But it had been an accident! He didn't want to marry her, but he certainly would never *push her off a cliff* to get out of it! Oh god, was that what they would think? His father and brothers? No, they couldn't—well, his father, maybe, but not Blaine and Lance! They couldn't—at least, Lance wouldn't?

*How am I going to tell them? How am I going to tell her father, her* sisters, *that I killed—*

A glimpse of movement caught his eye and he looked up.

Gwendolyn was walking toward him down the hall, carrying a bowl of popcorn.

# CHAPTER 14

## GWENDOLYN

Gwen focused on her breathing as she walked back down the hall. Earlier in the day, she'd thought she'd been totally ready to face Frederick. She'd come home, greeted the front-door guards as they carefully avoided eye contact, taken her time washing up and getting ready. She'd felt perfectly calm as she picked out one of her favorite dresses—a soft, flowing, seafoam-green one with long, drapey sleeves and a dark-green sash that tied at the waist—and put on a delicate gold necklace with a pretty orange stone pendant. She'd brushed her hair and slipped on a cute pair of dark-green shoes that matched the sash. Then she went down to the parlor to wait for the princes with Papa and her sisters.

And then they heard the sound of footsteps coming up the

main stairs, and Gwen was suddenly overcome with nervousness. She'd practically jumped out of her skin when King Leland burst through the door yelling, "Jack! Get over here, you old crusty noodle!"

They'd all been temporarily distracted after that, even Gwen, because Papa and King Leland were hugging and smiling and gushing about chess and armory mood boards and calling each other silly nicknames, and that was all pretty weird to watch. It was like both men had suddenly become schoolboys again. But of course it was wonderful to see Papa so happy, and the brief impression she got of King Leland was that he was very loud but also very friendly and fond of her father.

Then King Leland had instructed his sons to show the girls a great evening, and he and Papa had gone off to look at the armory, leaving the girls alone with the princes. At that point, Gwen finally realized that someone was missing.

"Where's Frederick?" she asked.

"Don't worry, Gwendolyn," Blaine had said reassuringly. "He's just running a little late."

"Yeah, and you'll never guess why he's late!" Lance began. "He's taking a lla—" But he broke off as Blaine jabbed him in the ribs with an elbow.

"Taking a lah?" Lorena asked, confused.

"Errr," Lance said. "Taking a . . . long pee! Frederick's late because he's taking a long pee right now."

"Mm-kay," Lorena said dubiously.

Gwen was aware that this was a very strange and overly personal excuse for being late but was also too nervous at that point to think straight. She was actually shaking! She needed to get a grip before Frederick arrived.

She stood up abruptly. "I'm gonna prepare some snacks for us. I'll be right back!" Then she dashed out the door, barely hearing Maria thanking her as she left.

She ran up the stairs to her private kitchen. *Popcorn*, she thought. *I'll just make some nice popcorn.* She wanted to make pies, pies were the *best* for calming anxiety, but that would take way too long.

She made the popcorn as slowly as she could, poured it into a bowl, then sprinkled it with freshly ground pastel-pink rock salt. No butter, though, since that would just get messy and Molly would *not* appreciate greasy fingerprint stains on the sofas.

It had helped a lot. She was still nervous, but she thought she could hold herself together now. *It will be fine*, she told herself as she headed back to the parlor. *You were looking forward to talking to Frederick now that you have Syrah's words to guide you, remember?* Did she remember? She ran over the key phrases again in her mind.

Syrah had advised her to start by telling Frederick she wanted him to know that she'd overheard what he'd said. Then . . . mention that he'd hurt her feelings, but that she understood . . . and what was the last part? Oh right. That she was fine not being his fiancé, and she'd happily watch from the sidelines as his friend and sister-in-law, and that she wanted him and everyone in both their families to be happy. *Oof.* That last part was a mouthful. But as long as she got the gist of it across, it would be okay. She'd just have to trust that the right words would come to her when she needed them.

Anyway, she still had some time to mentally prepare. Frederick hadn't even arrived yet. And once he did arrive, she'd have to wait until she was able to get a moment alone with him, so it could be a while.

Then she glanced up and saw him standing at the end of the hall.

She pulled awkwardly to a stop. *No,* was all she could think. *No, I'm not ready!*

But she had to be. She had to do this so their families could move forward. She made herself start walking again, tried to make her face find some normal, not-terrified expression. *You can do this,* she told herself. *And no crying! You need to be strong to do this right!*

# CHAPTER 15

## FREDERICK

*Wh—wh—what . . . ?! How—* He was caught between elation and bewilderment, paralyzed with shock. How could she be alive? Was it somehow *not* Gwendolyn who fell off the cliff? Had he murdered someone *else*?

She saw him at the same time, and she froze too. For a second she looked frightened, and then she seemed to steel herself. She walked forward purposefully.

"Hey, Gwendolyn!" he said. "You seem alive! Er—I mean, lively!" She didn't say anything. He waved at her inanely. "Uh, Gwen?"

She screwed up her face like she was struggling with some intense emotion. Then she raised her chin and looked him directly in the eye. "Hey, Frederick," she said in a strange, strained voice. "I know what you did to me."

*Oh god. It* was *her that I pushed off the cliff. But—but how did she survive that fall?*

"I'm sorry!" he whispered. "I'm sorry!"

She didn't seem to even hear him. "It hurt. It hurt a lot. But I want you to know that I'm okay."

*Is she—is she telling me that she's immortal? I don't understand what is happening!*

She fixed him with an even more intense stare and smiled at him with those frightening, pointed teeth. "Let's be friends, Frederick," she purred terrifyingly. "From now on, I'll be watching you from the shadows. I hope you're happy."

She walked away, but just before she disappeared through the doorway into the parlor, she looked back. Her grin widened, showing more teeth than he thought a regular human person should really have.

Frederick slid to the floor.

*She's a witch. She has to be. It's the only explanation.* He clutched at his stupid uniform collar, which suddenly felt way too tight. He was not marrying a witch! They couldn't make him. They—

"Okay, Frederick, I'm here," Blaine said, emerging from the door Gwendolyn had just vanished through. "What's up? Why are you on the floor?"

Frederick struggled to his feet and grabbed Blaine's uniform jacket desperately. "Gw-gw-Gwendolyn. She's . . . she's alive. But . . . earlier . . ."

"Yeah," Blaine said, peeling Frederick's fingers off of him with obvious distaste. "I can't understand you when you're hyperventilating like that. Can we be done here? The girls want us to take them to the amusement park in town."

"What? No, I—"

"Let's go. Whatever your objections are, they're overruled. But, boy, you still smell like Laverne."

"No! Blaine, wait!"

But Blaine, of course, did not wait. He dragged Frederick back into the parlor. "Okay!" he announced brightly. "We're all here. Let's go to the fair!"

The girls and Lance all cheered.

"Can I come too?" someone asked.

They all turned to see Prince Jamie, awake and sparkling, leaning through the hallway door.

"Jamie!" Lorena said. "You're back from work!"

Blaine let go of Frederick so that he could step forward to greet the newcomer. "Prince Jamie! It is an honor to finally meet you."

Jamie flashed a beautiful smile. It really wasn't fair how attractive he was. "It's nice to meet you guys too!"

"Bro, that wake of yours was amazing," Lance said. "Could I get added to a mailing list for them or something?"

Jamie's beautiful smile metamorphosed into a beautiful laugh. "I like you guys. You're funny."

Blaine returned to Frederick's side, probably to make sure he didn't run off. "Hey, speaking of you smelling like Laverne, where did you park her?"

"Um, about that," Frederick began. He still had to confess that part, too, that he'd let their father's beloved pet run off to who knew where. But before he could continue, the girls opened the parlor's main doors to reveal Laverne lounging on the other side.

Lorena tilted her head. "Is that a llama?" she asked.

"Uh, yes," Blaine said, being the first to recover, as usual. "Princesses, please meet Laverne, official llama of the Plaid Kingdom."

The squeal that erupted from all four Pastel siblings was enough to pierce the strongest eardrums. Even Lance winced. They all rushed forward to surround Laverne, petting her soft wool and murmuring words of admiration. Laverne took it all in happily, but it was clear that she had instantly fallen in love with Prince Jamie in particular. She nuzzled her head into his chest.

"Aw, hi, Laverne! I'm Jamie, and you're the most beautiful llama I've ever seen."

Laverne bleated in near ecstasy.

Frederick leaned against the wall, waiting for the lovefest to end so they could leave. There was no way Blaine would let him stay behind, so he tried to resign himself to going along and just doing his best to avoid being alone with Gwendolyn. When he looked at her now, giving the llama tentative little pets and laughing with her siblings, she was nothing like the horrifying creature she'd been in the hallway. She seemed almost normal. But maybe witches could do that—change their appearances and voices and how they were perceived. It had to be something like that; he couldn't possibly have imagined her threatening words and demeanor. She'd been absolutely terrifying.

Maybe he'd get the opportunity to talk to Blaine again at the fair. Or maybe he could talk to Lance, and Lance could talk to Blaine. And then Blaine could talk to Father. He'd find a way to make them understand. He wasn't giving up on getting out of this yet.

## CHAPTER 16

### GWENDOLYN

When the carriage let them off at the gates to the kingdom's local amusement park, Gwen stood for a moment and stared. Her sisters stopped beside her, equally transfixed. They'd been a bit nervous about leaving the palace—Papa would certainly never have allowed it had they asked. But the boys had pointed out that King Leland had told them to have a great night, and King Jack hadn't objected, and anyway the two of them would be off playing chess for hours. Gwen had still felt a little guilty as they headed out, but now she was very glad they'd agreed to go. The scene before them was positively magical.

Pink, white, and purple tents sprawled across the fairgrounds, each one sporting a center pole that flew a festive purple banner.

Along the perimeter, strings of tiny lights twinkled invitingly against the backdrop of the violet-swirled sunset sky. There were booths with games and prizes, some with savory food and fizzy drinks, and some offering brightly colored candy and other treats. A larger tent in the center had open sides that revealed an enchanting merry-go-round that Gwen instantly wanted to try out. Cheerful music floated through the air, and everywhere people were strolling and laughing and generally having a wonderful time.

"This is what amusement parks are like?" Lorena asked finally, her voice full of wonder.

Blaine turned to look at them. "You all have really never been to an amusement park before?"

Maria shrugged. "I've read about them in books and magazines, and dreamed of getting to go one day, but Father never lets us actually go anywhere. So if you guys have suggestions for what we should do, please tell us!"

Blaine and Lance exchanged a knowing glance that Gwen couldn't quite decipher. "I know the perfect place to start," Blaine said. "Follow me."

Gwen let the others walk slightly ahead, Frederick among them. He'd been silent in the carriage, but she was starting to feel certain that he was just a way quieter person than his brash and bold older brothers. She felt so much better after talking to him back in the palace. She couldn't wait to tell Syrah and the others how well their plan had worked, even though she hadn't spoken quite as eloquently as she'd meant to—he'd surprised her, standing there in the hall, and she had *not* been ready for that conversation to happen right then!

But she'd known she had to seize the moment, and that was exactly what she'd done. She was really proud of herself for pushing through her fear. She hadn't managed to say all of Syrah's suggested phrases exactly right, but she'd gotten her meaning across, and that was all that really mattered. Frederick had seemed stunned by her mature and measured response, just like the cursed princesses had predicted. And now she and Frederick could work on just being friends and supportive siblings-in-law with no unwanted engagement hanging over their heads.

"Hey, Gwennie." Jamie stepped up beside her. He was holding a giant blue cloud of cotton candy that he must have just purchased. She couldn't help laughing; it was as big as his head! "Want a bite?"

"Sure." She leaned over and took an experimental nibble. The blue fluff melted to sugar at once, filling her mouth with an intense, slightly artificial-tasting sweetness. "Yum!"

"I know we've both been pretty busy lately, and we haven't gotten to talk much over the past week," Jamie said. "But I've been meaning to ask you for a while now . . . has everything been okay with you?"

For a second, she was startled—and then she just felt foolish. Of course she couldn't hide anything from Jamie! "I guess you knew something was off once you ate the waffle I made for you, huh?"

"Actually, funny story." He offered her another bite of cotton candy, but she shook her head. "So, of course you know how my taste buds allow me to discern not only the exact ingredients of a dish, but also the emotions of the person who prepared the food. What you may not know, however, is that there are occasional flavors and emotions that taste nearly identical to my tongue. Like schadenfreude and fried potatoes. I always mix those up."

"Oh! I had no idea."

"It happens rarely, and I keep a journal of flavor crossovers to help me stay aware. But one of my few crucial blind spots is that emotional devastation tastes identical to carpet. I once wrote a terrible review of a chef from the Paisley Kingdom because I thought he had served me Bolognese that fell on the floor. Turns out, his beloved parakeet had just passed away." He shook his head sadly. "It's the grease stain on my conscience that will never wash out." Then he brightened and took another bite of cotton candy. "Anyway, when you made me that waffle after my wake, all I thought I tasted was carpet. But I should have known you would never serve me something that fell on the floor!" He laughed.

Gwen couldn't meet his eye. "Um, well, actually—"

"But then when you baked us those cookies for game night, I definitely tasted a lot of new emotions that I've never experienced in your cooking before. So I know something must be going on with you. I won't pry, but if there's ever anything you want to talk about, I'm here."

Jamie really was the best. Gwen leaned over and gave him a quick hug, careful not to get cotton candy in her hair. "Thank you, Jamie. I was carrying a lot of anxiety about my engagement to Prince Frederick. I . . . I knew he wasn't interested in me as a potential fiancé."

"What?!"

"No, it's okay! I just talked with him and told him that we don't need to move forward with our engagement. We can just be friends! So, I don't have to feel awkward around him anymore. And all that's left is to convince Maria and Lorena to get married without me. Which hopefully won't be too hard, given how they talk about the princes." She sighed happily. "It's all going to be fine now."

"Well, it's not fine with me!" Jamie said, his tone furious. "He hasn't even gotten to know you yet! I'm going to talk to him."

"What? No, Jamie! Please! You don't have to do that." She had *just* made everything okay with Frederick—she didn't want Jamie to stir things back up!

"Okay, okay. If you say so," Jamie said. He took a few more bites of blue fluff as they caught up to the others.

Lance was standing in front of a scary-looking house with a bunch of fake bats outside and weird faces peeking from some of the windows. A huge banner above the door had the words

DISGUSTING BLOODY CLOWN MURDERHOUSE printed in dripping red letters. Lorena and Maria stared at the sign with wide eyes.

"Murderhouse?" Lorena said. "I don't want to go in there!"

"The magazines never mentioned anything like this," Maria said. "Aren't there, like, ponies or something we could go to see instead? Or we passed some really cute little shops that were selling these adorable figurines, we could go back—"

"Oh, but this is a quintessential part of the amusement park experience," Blaine said. "It would really be a crime for you to miss it. Just take my hand, and I promise to keep you safe."

Maria blushed prettily. "Oh . . . all right, then."

Lance turned to Lorena. "Come on, it'll be fun," he said. "And if you get scared, these arms are ready for you anytime." He held them up oddly, extended with his palms facing the sky, like he was carrying something. Or someone.

"Why are you holding them out like that?" Lorena asked.

Lance glanced down at his hands and then dropped them to his sides. "Never mind. Let's go!"

Gwen thought the house looked kind of like the front of Cursed Princess Club headquarters. (The inside and the back of the CPC house were lovely, but the front was run-down and kind of spooky. Probably to discourage unwanted visitors, Gwen assumed.) Somehow that made the murderhouse feel a lot less scary, although the shapes and faces that occasionally passed by the windows were definitely giving her the creeps. But she was willing to be a good sport. It was supposed to fun, right? "Well, Jamie? Shall we—?"

But Jamie wasn't standing next to her anymore.

"Jamie?"

She whirled around, looking for him. And then she saw him, standing beside Frederick, one arm thrown companionably over the other prince's shoulders.

"Hey, guys!" Jamie said. "Me and Frederick are going to go have some bonding time, so go on without us, okay?"

"We're what?" Frederick asked. It was clear he hadn't been actively involved in making that plan. Gwen fought down her momentary unease. Jamie wasn't going to say anything about what they'd discussed. He probably really did just want to get to know Frederick better. He must have picked up on the fact that Frederick was pretty shy and wanted to try to draw him out in a one-on-one conversation. Jamie was really sweet that way.

"Okay, have fun!" Maria said.

"We'll see you after!" Gwen added. She didn't want to act like she minded, in case it made Frederick think she hadn't meant what she said about just being friends. She *didn't* mind. She just didn't want Jamie to say more than she was comfortable with. But she would just have to trust her brother.

Jamie waved and steered Frederick to the next building over, which was an indoor boat ride called The Perfect Relation-Ship. He probably figured it would be nice and quiet in there. They ducked through the red curtain covering the heart-shaped entrance. Frederick gave them all one last panicked glance and disappeared.

Blaine and Lance led the rest of them up to the front door of the murderhouse. In the entryway, a sad clown in a pink-and-white striped outfit greeted them in a morose monotone. "Welcome. Please enjoy each of the ten disgustingly bloody rooms we've prepared."

"Uh, thank you," said Lorena, leaning away from him.

"Blaine, I don't know about this," Maria said.

"Don't worry, Maria. Just stay close to me if you get scared."

Maria nodded, moving closer to him, and Gwen had to hide a smile. She'd finally caught on; the boys thought the girls would get scared and turn to them for comfort and cuddling. It hardly seemed necessary, since Maria and Lorena were obviously both infatuated with their princes already, but Gwen supposed it was harmless. It was just a silly amusement park attraction, after all. Besides, how scary could a bunch of random clowns be?

They walked slowly into the first room. It was dark and creepy, with a black-and-white tiled floor and splatters of what looked like blood on the walls. All the room seemed to contain was a pile of old wooden crates, though. Wasn't there supposed to be a disgusting bloody tableau of some kind?

Gwen approached the crates to look at them more closely.

"Do you see something?" Lorena whispered.

"I—" Gwen broke off. "Did you hear that?"

~ 168 ~

A stealthy rustling was coming from behind the crates.

The girls froze, trying to listen. Gwen's heartbeat felt very loud inside her body.

Suddenly a terrifying clown with glowing yellow eyes and long, sharp fangs leapt from behind the crates, shouting "Give me your blood!"

Maria, Lorena, and Gwen all screamed. "Aaaaah! Vampire clown!"

Blaine stepped toward Maria, arms out, ready to capitalize on his chance to comfort her. Maria turned to him and vomited on his shoes. (Maria always vomited in pretty pastel rainbow colors, so it was a little less gross than it might have been, but it was still gross.)

Meanwhile, Lorena had dropped automatically into a fighting stance and kicked out one leg to smash the clown in the face. He fell with a grunt and landed at Gwen's feet.

Gwen had calmed down once she remembered this was just an actor pretending to be a vampire clown, not the real thing. Now she was just concerned. She leaned down over the fallen man. "Oh my gosh, do you need help, mister?"

"Scram, kid," he muttered, his face pressed into the dirty floor. "I just want to be left alone so no one can see me like this." In a quieter voice he added woefully, "I hate my job."

"Oh, okay," Gwen said, a little doubtfully. She tried to hide her worry, since he didn't seem to want sympathy right now, and forced her voice to be bright and cheerful. It seemed to be helping, because he lifted his face from the floor and turned to look up at her. She flashed him a big toothy smile, just like the one she'd given Frederick after their talk. "Don't worry. I can make sure no one finds your body for a long time."

The clown made a gurgling sound and then passed out.

*Oh no! He must really be hurt,* Gwen thought. *I'll find some medics once we get out of here.* For now, though, she went over to Maria and handed her a crumpled (but clean!) tissue from her pocket. "Are you okay?"

Maria nodded, wiping delicately at her face. "I'm just so embarrassed."

"It's not your fault," Lorena said. "That guy was really good at his job! I thought he was a real vampire clown for a second there too. We just react differently to violent supernatural threats, that's all." She took an experimental step on her kicking foot and winced. "I think I sprained something."

Blaine was looking grimly at his pastel-vomit-spattered boots. "This wasn't really what I had in mind," he said.

Lance seemed a bit shaken as well, perhaps not having been aware of Lorena's extensive martial arts training. "Maybe we should all just find an exit."

Gwen thought Lance was probably right, but there was a problem. She pointed to a sign above their heads that said NO EXIT UNTIL THE END OF THE HAUNTED HOUSE.

"We've made a huge mistake," Blaine announced solemnly.

"Yeah," Lorena agreed.

"Well," Maria said, wiping at the pastel vomit on her dress. "Only nine disgusting bloody murder clown rooms to go!"

# CHAPTER 17

## FREDERICK

Frederick perched at the very edge of the pale-pink, heart-shaped seat in the hot-pink little boat with its giant, decorative, heart-emblazoned sail and its tiny, also decorative, also heart-emblazoned captain's wheel. The walls were purple and the water was sparkly lavender and there were streamers of hearts and flowers dangling from the ceiling. Soft, romantic music emanated from everywhere and nowhere, swirling around them with invisible, alluring intensity. The air smelled like roses. The boat rocked gently as it progressed deeper into the pink-hued tunnel. Prince Jamie sat beside him, perfectly matching the decor and apparently totally at ease despite the aggressive love themes attacking them from all sides.

"Why did we go on this ride, of all things?" Frederick asked, not quite turning to look at Jamie.

"I just headed for the nearest building," Jamie admitted. "But this is actually perfect for getting to chat with my future brother-in-law!"

Frederick didn't say anything. What could he say? That he had no intention of marrying into the Pastel family? He supposed he'd technically still be Jamie's brother-in-law if his brothers married Maria and Lorena, but he knew that wasn't what Jamie meant. Of course, his intentions didn't seem to matter very much to anyone anyway. He knew his father was going to force him to go through with the marriage. King Leland wouldn't care if Gwendolyn was a witch. He wouldn't care if she was a giant, three-headed, venomous scorpion! Frederick was trapped, like he was always trapped. Trapped by his father's rigidity and his mother's emotional distance and his responsibilities as a Plaid prince. Trapped most of all by his own inferiority, his helplessness to change his own destiny. What would have happened if Blaine had been the one engaged to Gwendolyn? Would he have been able to stand up to Father? But no—Blaine would do what was best for the kingdom without complaint. It was just one more way that he was better than Frederick.

The silence was stretching on too long. He had to say something; he couldn't risk offending Jamie. If word got back to his father that he was being anything less than a perfect guest—

"Listen," Jamie said. "I know that you and Gwen talked, and that things are at a bit of a dead end right now."

*More like an* undead *end*, Frederick couldn't help thinking. He braced himself for Jamie's anger, which was surely forthcoming. If Gwen had told him what had happened, no wonder Jamie wanted to get him somewhere alone. So there would be no witnesses to whatever he was about to do in retaliation.

But Jamie's next words surprised him. "No one should be forced to get close to anyone that they don't want to," he said, his tone still calm and kind. "But please allow me just to say that Gwen is truly special. Everyone who comes to know her feels that way, but I know her better than anyone else."

Frederick risked a glance at Jamie. The other prince's pretty eyes were practically brimming with sincerity. "This may seem like an odd segue, but you know I'm a food critic, right? A really famous and successful one, if I do say so myself. I can learn a lot from someone's cooking. Way more than you might imagine. I've tried dishes by chefs all over the world, and I've never yet tasted anything as lovely and warm as the food Gwen makes. There's something wonderful about her and everything she puts her heart into. So, I guess what I'm saying is, I'm looking forward to the day you realize this too."

Now Frederick was at a loss for words again, but this time for entirely different reasons. Jamie really seemed to love his sister. Could he somehow not know she was a witch? Or did he not care? Or—could Frederick have been wrong, somehow?

Jamie smiled, sparkling a little in that strange way he had. "But the point of this ride is to get to know *you* better, Frederick!"

Frederick blinked. He was having a little trouble keeping up. "Huh? It is?"

"Tell me what your hobbies are!" Jamie leaned forward as though he literally could not be more interested in any other topic, ever.

"What? Oh . . . um, I—I don't really have time for any." *I'm too busy being forced into engagements and dragging llamas from one kingdom to another*, he thought bitterly.

"Oh, come on," Jamie said, turning up the sparkle even more. "Everyone has things they enjoy. Or at least used to enjoy?" He leaned even closer, his sparkly light growing blinding.

Frederick squinted and held up a hand to block the glare. "Uh, okay—fine. Reading. I like reading books. I mean, I used to. I built model ships when I was younger too."

"Ooh, how refined! That must take a lot of patience and care."

It did. It had, anyway. He hadn't touched his models in years. Not since—well, he just hadn't.

Jamie seemed to finally pick up on the fact that Frederick was not enjoying this conversation. Or—more likely, given how perceptive Jamie seemed to be—he was finally going to take pity on Frederick and stop trying to make him talk. "Um, okay, Frederick. Just one more question."

"Okay." *Thank goodness.* All he wanted was to sit in silence until the ride was finally over.

Jamie leaned in even closer, which was really too close by any normal person's standard. "Have you ever been attracted to someone?"

"What?" *Oh god, does he know somehow? About the portrait?* Could he know what they'd all thought when they first saw it? That *Jamie* was Frederick's intended bride? Frederick shot to his feet in panic, some deep flight instinct making him want to run from his humiliation. Underneath him, he felt the boat pitch wildly. "*It was an honest mistake!*"

"Mistake?" Jamie's confusion was quickly overtaken by concern. "Frederick, please sit down, you're rocking the—"

But it was too late. Frederick realized it with a sinking heart just before the boat flipped sideways and they both plunged with a sparkly splash into the lavender, rose-scented water.

~

Frederick should have known from the start that he could never outrun humiliation. It was always there, waiting to pounce gleefully upon him.

The amusement park staff had had to stop the boat ride in order to safely pull the two princes out of the water. They were led out through the ride's heart-shaped entrance, sopping wet, with stray flower petals in their hair, while what seemed to be literally every last person at the park stared and, probably, covertly laughed.

They met up with the rest of their little party, who had apparently suffered some mishaps of their own. Maria's dress and Blaine's boots were splattered with what looked like dried rainbow vomit, Lorena was limping and leaning heavily on Lance in order to walk, and Gwendolyn—well, Gwendolyn was the only one who looked somewhat okay, if visibly concerned for her sisters. Frederick tried to be cheered by the fact that his brothers' obvious plan to use the scary clown house to get closer to the girls had *severely* misfired, but he was too chilled and soggy to take much comfort even from that.

Someone summoned the carriage, and they rode back to the Pastel Palace in miserable silence. Molly led them wordlessly to the living room, where an agitated King Jack leapt to his feet as soon as he saw them.

"What in the devil happened to all of you?!" he shouted.

They all looked at one another, no one wanting to be the first to try to explain. And then Lorena abruptly started laughing. Her sisters joined her, and then Lance and Blaine also burst into helpless hysterics. Frederick found himself chuckling as well, as the absurdity of the whole night hit him all at once. There they were, standing before their king-fathers, wet, filthy, publicly embarrassed, and not one of them could do anything but dissolve into decidedly un-royal-sounding snorts and giggles.

Molly finally intervened, shooing the still-laughing younger generation toward baths while ordering tea for the kings. King Jack still looked vaguely like he wanted to kill someone, but he seemed more worried and bemused than angry at this point. King Leland seemed entirely unconcerned.

Frederick let the servants help him out of his wet clothes and into a hot tub, which felt heavenly after the chilly ride home. They brought him a set of Jamie's clothes to put on afterward, which were not exactly his style, but the purple pants and white top were clean and dry, and the pink sweater that went over them was delightfully cozy and warm. He would have been feeling almost entirely better, except that he'd begun sneezing sometime after they got back. Being shivery and wet for so long, in addition to his immersion in that filthy boat-ride water—it had not been nearly as nice underneath that sparkly surface—had apparently given him a cold. He'd thought incubation periods were usually a bit longer than that, but who knew what weird germs he could have been exposed to during his dunking? And maybe Pastel pathogens were super fast-acting. You could never really know how things worked in other people's kingdoms.

So now he was surreptitiously sniffling as he sat with the others around the fireplace, catching up the kings on their night. Not that Frederick himself was contributing anything to the conversation. His bad mood had returned in full force, and he wanted no part of any of this. He was sure no one would care what he had to say anyway.

"Oh, Father," Maria was saying, "we had so much fun! Although I'm mortified that I vomited in front of you, Blaine!"

Blaine took her hand and patted it comfortingly. "Please don't worry, Maria. I can honestly say that somehow even your vomit is beautiful. As well as quite patriotic!"

Maria blinked her long lashes at him. "Oh, Blaine, I'm definitely ready to spend the rest of my life with you!"

King Jack seemed taken aback by that. "M-my, you two already seem so comfortable with each other . . . "

"Daddy!" Lorena interrupted. "I KO'd like eight murder-clowns!"

"It was pretty sexy," Lance said, "after it stopped being terrifying."

King Jack was twitching a bit now. "Yes, very—very nice, sweetie."

Frederick attempted to tune out the rest of this intolerable conversation. He had tried to rally, to be a good sport, but he just couldn't do it. This visit to the Pastel Kingdom was even worse than the first had been! He'd had an exhausting journey with Laverne, then that horrific encounter with Gwendolyn, and then that awkward private chat with Jamie followed by falling into filthy amusement park water! And just to top it all off, now he was feeling sick too.

He hated getting sick. No one in the Plaid Kingdom was exactly nurturing or comforting when you weren't feeling well. You still even had to do push-ups if you were the last one to the table. Which you probably would be, since you were sick. He'd heard stories of sick people who got to stay in bed and be waited on by those who loved them, but those were probably just more stupid fairy tales based on lies and wishful thinking.

"Um, here." A steaming bowl of soup suddenly appeared in front of him. He looked up to see Gwen holding it out to him. He hadn't even noticed that she'd left the room in the first place, let alone that she'd returned with soup.

"What's this?"

She shrugged as well as she could while holding out the bowl. "You were starting to look a little ill, so I thought I'd make you some soup."

He was so surprised, he forgot to be afraid of her. He took the bowl from her hands. "You—you *made* this? For me?"

She blushed and sat on the couch beside him, not meeting his eye. "It's not anything fancy! And you don't have to eat it if you don't want to."

He looked into the bowl. Brightly colored bits of vegetables floated in a shimmery golden broth. It smelled incredible. He couldn't remember the last time anyone other than a kitchen servant had made a meal for him. And never *just* for him. Why would she do this after everything that had happened earlier that day? Could it be poisoned? He tried to feel alarm at the thought, but the smell of the soup overcame all his efforts at panicking.

Maybe he'd just take a sip. To be polite.

He lifted the spoon to his lips and tasted it.

*My god.*

He closed his eyes, needing to focus entirely on what was happening in his mouth. Such warmth. Not just the temperature, but the flavors, the texture, and after he swallowed, the feeling he had in his stomach . . . How could he describe it? The soup tasted like kindness. Was this what Jamie had been talking about at the amusement park? *But how? How could this be from the same person who . . . who . . .*

He opened his eyes and looked at his bowl. He'd eaten every last drop.

"Thank you, Gwendolyn," he said. "Your soup was really amazing." *Amazing* was an understatement. He didn't think he'd ever tasted anything that good in maybe ever.

"Oh, I'm glad! I hope you feel better!" She was smiling, and it was a nice smile this time. Not that scary one from earlier.

He did feel better. His sniffles were gone, but more than that . . . he felt comforted . . . and relaxed, and . . .

He closed his eyes again. He was so sleepy. He'd just rest for a minute. Dimly, he heard the others still droning on, talking about the marriages, wanting to make them happen as soon as possible. He should be worried about that, too, about having to get married, but he couldn't—he just didn't want to worry about anything right now. He felt too good to worry about anything.

Suddenly—was it suddenly?—he was aware that everything had gone very quiet. He was resting his head on something soft.

He blinked his eyes open, feeling groggy. "Oh, I'm sorry—did I doze off?" He lifted his head . . .

. . . to find his face inches from Gwen's face, his eyes staring into hers.

*Oh . . . oh, no.* The soft thing he'd been sleeping on had been her shoulder. He became aware of the rest of his body, which was leaning pretty cozily against hers. Had his *lips* been resting against her *neck?* He flushed, and saw that she was just as startled and embarrassed as he was. As one, they slowly turned to look at the others.

Everyone was staring at them. For several long seconds, no one said a word.

Then Lorena whispered, "Dang, Gwen."

And King Leland added, "Attaboy, son."

Frederick turned back to Gwendolyn. "I—I'm so sorry! I didn't m-mean to—"

She was staring at her hands folded in her lap, her face bright red. "N-no, it's okay!"

King Jack stood up, his face distorted with rage. Glaring at Frederick and Gwen, his hands crushed into fists, he yelled, "*I'm postponing the weddings!*"

Frederick barely heard the rest of the heated conversation that followed—the older girls passionately objecting, his father questioning, King Jack shouting about everything moving too fast, everyone hurrying to end the evening and regroup to figure out what was next. He was too mortified. But once they were in the carriage headed home, Laverne smushed in awkwardly across his brothers' thighs, there was no way to avoid his father's gaze. His father's *admiring* gaze. Why was he looking at Frederick that way?

"I've got to hand it to you, Frederick. I gave you an order to express your devotion to Gwendolyn, and you really came through. It was, perhaps, a little too forward, to our detriment, but that's all right. I was moved nonetheless."

"Huh?" Frederick gaped at him. "No, that's not what happened, I—"

Lance kicked him in the shin from across the carriage. "Don't act so shy, li'l bro. That was a bold move, nuzzling all up on—" Thankfully, Laverne chose that moment to shift farther onto Lance's lap, which distracted him from finishing that horrid statement.

"Why, exactly, is Laverne in the carriage with us?" Blaine asked around a faceful of wool.

Father laughed. "Sorry, boys. Frederick won tonight, so I decided we'd all take the carriage home together. Anyhow, I'm proud of you, my boy. Keep up the good work."

It wasn't fair. Frederick never heard words like that from his father. *Never.* Proud of him? Usually Father was only too happy to tell him what a disappointment he was. And now he was being praised for accidentally falling asleep on Gwen's shoulder, which the rest of his family seemed to think was some calculated act to show her how much he liked her. It was a relief to be back in his father's good graces, but this was not the way he'd wanted to do it. And now he was only more enmeshed in the triple marriage plans.

He turned his face to the window, opting out of any further conversation. He tried to think about what he could possibly do to extricate himself from this mess, but somehow his mind kept returning to those moments before he came fully awake, that feeling of warmth and safety and softness as he rested his head on Gwen's shoulder.

# CHAPTER 18

## GWENDOLYN

Gwen slipped into her nightgown, feeling like the day could not have gone any better. Okay, yes, there had been all that shouting at the end, and before that, the unfortunate events at the amusement park, but before any of those other things, she had had the confrontation with Frederick, and the relief of having that over with—and knowing it had gone so well!—made her feel like a giant weight had been lifted from her chest. She could almost relax again! All that was left was to talk to her family tomorrow. *I'll tell them that Frederick and I both support the union of our families, but we'd be happier just to be friends.*

Unbidden, the image of Frederick's face, so close to hers, came suddenly to her mind. His lovely green eyes had been inches from her own, blinking at her in adorable confusion. Of course it hadn't been on purpose; he'd simply fallen asleep—no wonder, after that ordeal he'd endured with Jamie—and he surely hadn't meant to rest his head on her shoulder with his lips brushing her neck. She flushed a little again now, thinking about it. She hadn't known what to do, so she'd done nothing, just let him sleep. It had felt so nice, his body resting against hers. She'd been so happy that he'd liked the soup and that he'd seemed pleased she'd made it for him, and clearly he'd needed the rest, and really, there was nothing scandalous about someone's head on your shoulder. She didn't know why her family had reacted the way they had.

Well, she supposed she knew why Papa had reacted so strongly. After all his hard work to keep them away from boys their entire lives until now, it must have been a shock to see one actually touching her, even in such an innocent way. And she could tell he was having mixed feelings about how quickly her sisters' courtships were progressing. He had probably imagined it would take them much longer to get to know one another. But that was just Papa being Papa. He would calm down eventually, and once he saw how unhappy it would make Maria and Lorena to postpone the weddings, he would surely agree to make them happen sooner.

But either way, she and Frederick would just be friends. She tried to bring back the feeling of relief at having that matter settled, but instead her mind tried to reconjure that unexpected moment of closeness, that image of Frederick's sweet face looking at her, his beautiful eyes, his soft lips . . .

Gwen grabbed her brush and sat down at her vanity. She must be really exhausted! Her mind was too tired to think straight. She'd just get ready for bed really quickly, and in the morning everything would be clear again. She began to brush out her hair and glanced up at the mirror.

And then dropped her brush with a gasp.

Her image in the mirror was—broken. Instead of her face, she only saw a shattered black void.

~

Gwen woke to warm sunlight and the familiar feel of Mr. Possum's teeth gently digging into her scalp. She smiled and stretched, careful not to disturb Mr. Rat, who was still snoring beside her. She disengaged Mr. Possum from her hair (they'd come to an agreement that she'd let him sleep there as long as he didn't make it difficult to extract him in the morning) and rubbed his fuzzy belly as she shook off the last of her sleepiness. She felt oddly relieved that it was morning; did she have a bad dream last night or something?

She slipped out of bed, still trying to remember what she might have dreamed about. Maybe something about that ridiculous clown murderhouse? Then she passed by her mirror and froze, staring in bewilderment.

Right.

That's why she'd been feeling so uneasy.

Her reflection was shattered, just like it had been last night. She'd tried to believe she was just half asleep when it had happened the night before, that she'd just been seeing things, but she wasn't half asleep now.

Slowly, she reached toward the mirror. She could see her reflected arm moving, see her hand as it approached the glass. She could see almost everything except where her face should be. Her fingers touched the mirror's surface, and it was perfectly smooth. *But it must be broken in some way*, she thought. *Otherwise, what—*

"Father, you can't be serious!" Maria's outraged voice rang from the hallway.

Gwen whirled toward the door, part of her recognizing that she was only too happy to be pulled away from the mirror. She flung open her door. "What's going on? Is everything okay?"

"Oh! Morning, sweetie," Papa said, giving her a somewhat shaky smile. "I just made a little announcement, that's all! Your sisters are taking the news a bit dramatically."

Gwen took in her sisters' furious faces and narrowed her eyes at him. "What's the announcement?"

"Well, unfortunately, it looks like I must depart on another expedition with my troops, much sooner than I had planned. I have to leave this afternoon and will be gone for a few weeks."

"Oh," she said, surprised. "I mean, that's really sad news, and of course we'll miss you, Papa! But it's not like this is the first time this has happened—"

"Yes, it is sad news," Maria interrupted, "but that's not why we're upset. It's because of this!" She thrust a piece of parchment into Gwen's face. Maria was shaking it around angrily, but Gwen could just make out the words *A List of Fatherly Decrees* in large letters at the top.

Papa rolled his eyes. "It's simply a list of some new house rules! I just, uh, realized that I've been a bit too lenient with you girls!"

Lorena crossed her arms. "I'm pretty sure that's not true, Daddy."

"Me too," Maria agreed. "But either way, these rules are unacceptable!" She stopped shaking the parchment and read aloud. "'While Papa is gone, no daughters are allowed to see the Plaid princes nor let them inside of this palace.' Why, Father? Wasn't one of the reasons you wanted us to marry them so that they could keep us company while you're gone so often?"

"Those have always been the rules here," Father said. "You've never been allowed outside the palace grounds, and no one has ever been allowed to set foot in here while I'm gone. And until you are married, there will be no exemptions to these rules. Not even for the princes."

"But then why did you also push back the weddings?!" Maria said, her voice rising.

"Because you girls just aren't ready yet!" he yelled back. Gwen and her sisters exchanged glances. She thought they all knew who really wasn't ready.

Lorena snatched the parchment from Maria. "Okay, but that's not even the worst decree. Listen to this: 'During any interaction with the opposite sex, daughters shall only wear specific, father-approved attire.'" She raised an eyebrow at him. "What, exactly, is 'father-approved attire'?"

Papa sighed. "I expected pushback on this one, so I came prepared. Jamie, you can come out now!"

The door across the hall slowly creaked open. Jamie stepped out, his face a mask of mortification and irritation. His face was the only part of him they could actually see. The rest of him was enveloped in a puffy monstrosity of lavender fabric layered in voluminous tiers that went all the way down to the floor. A high white collar hid most of his neck, and a matronly bonnet covered most of his hair. Enormous bows of dark olive-green festooned the front of the dress and the back of the bonnet, with matching bands of green ribbon cinching the long sleeves into weird little sections down to the white lacy wrists.

"Papa," Gwen said carefully, "why would you make Jamie wear that?"

"What? I needed a model!" Papa gazed approvingly at his son. "And doesn't he look adorable? This dress shows that you can exude grace and femininity without needing to expose much skin!"

Jamie's face was turning an alarming shade of red. At first

Gwen thought he was just growing more and more embarrassed to be part of this ludicrous demonstration, but then Jamie whispered in a strained voice, "I . . . can't . . ."

And then he shouted, "Breathe!" as he tore the dress from his body, leaving him standing there in his pink bunny-print underwear.

Papa's eyebrows lowered in annoyance and disappointment. "Well, that backfired. Forget that rule, girls."

"Then can we get rid of this preposterous rule too?" Maria asked. "'No physical contact is ever allowed with the opposite sex, excluding family.' None, like, at all? Ever?"

"A nice compliment or curtsy can be just as affectionate as a love language."

Maria just stared at him, too incredulous to speak

"Daddy—" Lorena began.

"No more arguing, girls. Let's just cut to the chase and have you all promise to adhere to these rules, shall we?" He turned to Gwen. "Let's start with you, Gwennie-Pie. No physical contact or letting any princes put their face really close to yours. Promise Papa, okay?"

"Don't do it, Gwen!" Maria pleaded.

"Yeah, you don't have to agree to this!" said Lorena.

But Gwen had been struck by a great idea. A way to seize her moment to say what she needed to say and derail this insane rule conversation before Maria and Lorena completely lost their minds.

"Um, actually, this is the perfect opportunity to talk to all of you about something really important to me."

Everyone stopped arguing at once. "Of course, sweetie," Papa said. "What is it?"

Now that the moment was here, anxiety came clawing back up her chest. What if they were angry? What if they wouldn't accept her decision? What if—? But then she saw her siblings' kind, encouraging expressions, and her father's patient, inquiring one, and the anxiety dissipated. They were so ready to put everything else aside to listen to her. They loved her. They would understand.

"Um," she began. "I've been afraid to say this because the last thing I want is to ruin Maria's and Lorena's engagements, or to hurt our alliance with the Plaid Kingdom. But Frederick and I talked yesterday, and"—she took a breath and then said the next part all in a rush—"we'd like to cancel our engagement, as we both feel like there's no attraction between us."

For a second they all just looked at her. She searched their faces, trying to guess what they were feeling. At first, they all just seemed surprised. But then her sisters looked stricken.

"Oh, Gwennie," Maria said, coming forward and taking her hand. "Have we been rushing you? I think we forget sometimes that you're the youngest of all of us. All of these new pressures and emotions can be really confusing, I know."

"Yeah," said Lorena. "I guess we've been a little selfish, charging ahead so fast without considering whether it was too fast for you. I'm really sorry if we've made you feel unready."

Maria nodded. "Me too. And Gwen, you never have to worry about doing anything for our sake. Nothing you do will affect our decision to marry or not marry, just so long as we know you're happy."

"That's right, sweetie," Papa said, and Gwen nearly melted with relief, realizing his reaction was the one she'd been dreading most of all.

"But," Maria went on, "maybe don't call off the engagement altogether? Why don't we just slow things down and see how they go?"

"Yeah," said Lorena. "There's plenty of time! You don't actually have to decide anything right now."

Gwen bit her lip. All she'd been able to think about was getting her family to support her decision not to marry Frederick. It hadn't even occurred to her that she didn't have to decide anything permanent right now. Although . . . of course it *was* all decided, wasn't it? Frederick wasn't attracted to her. She wasn't ever going to agree to a marriage that wasn't something both people wanted. And she didn't . . . she didn't want it either. She just wanted to be his friend and sister-in-law. Her mind tried to show her the close-up image of Frederick's face from last night again, but she pushed it away. That hadn't meant anything.

"Um, okay," she said, knowing she had to say something. "Sure, that sounds fair." The important thing was that her sisters said they wouldn't call off their marriages. Even if she wasn't officially calling off her own engagement, she now knew that she *could*, when the time was right, and it wouldn't ruin everything. She and Frederick could still privately know that they weren't going to get married, even if they let the others think they were going to wait and see. And it wasn't strictly a lie—another lie—because, really, who knew? Maybe they would change their minds. *I mean, we won't, of course. But anything is possible, so letting my family think we could change our minds isn't lying. Even if I know we won't. Because we won't. Obviously.*

"Great," Maria said. "And, Father, we'll agree to slow things down with our engagements too. And we won't see the princes again until after you've returned."

"But we're not doing any of that other weird stuff you listed," Lorena said.

Father nodded his head gravely. "Thank you, girls. I appreciate it. But I must have you abide by one more rule before I leave."

"Another rule?!" Maria exclaimed.

"But, Daddy!" Lorena whined.

"The final rule," he said, using his sternest voice. "Always remember that Papa loves you." He smiled like he was joking, but Gwen saw the sincerity and vulnerability in his eyes. He really did want them to remember that, no matter what.

"We love you too!" they all cried in unison. And then they

gathered for a big group hug. Including Jamie, who was still in his underwear.

"Have a safe trip, Papa!" Gwen said, giving him an extra hug as the rest of them pulled away. "And Jamie, please go put on some clothes."

Jamie ran down the hall toward his room, shaking his pink, bunny-covered butt at them along the way. The laughter that followed was a welcome release after all of those intense emotions. Papa left them to finish preparing for his trip, Maria and Lorena headed downstairs to breakfast, and Gwen darted back to her own room to change out of her nightgown. She dressed quickly, telling herself she was just really hungry. The smell of Chef Martina's pancakes wafting up the stairs was enough to make anyone want to get to the table fast! That was the only reason she was hurrying so much that she didn't look in the mirror at all.

# CHAPTER 19

## GWENDOLYN

That afternoon, Gwen slung her bag over her shoulder and headed back downstairs. Today was a Cursed Princess Club day, and she was pleased to discover how much she was looking forward to seeing everyone.

Her sisters were lying upside down on the couch, legs hooked over the back and heads dangling off the cushions. Lorena was holding a book, but it was turned the wrong way around, so Gwen didn't think she was getting much reading done. Jamie and Miss Agatha stood nearby, looking worriedly at the girls.

"I want to see Blaine again," Maria was saying. "Is Father home from his expedition yet?"

"It's only been an hour since he left," Lorena said, "so probably not."

Maria pouted and looked miserably at the ceiling. "It's not fair. I miss him so much already!"

Miss Agatha suddenly brightened. "Girls, if you miss the princes that much, might I suggest writing them a letter?" She slipped effortlessly into her lecturing voice. "Throughout history, letter exchanges have been a creative and renowned practice for lovers to express their feelings for one another."

Lorena swung herself upright immediately. "Miss Agatha, you're a genius! Let's get started right away!"

Miss Agatha smiled. "Very good, Lorena! I like your proactive attitude!"

Maria was sitting right side up now too. "We can also send them little gifts to remember us by! It will be fun!"

"And we've got paper right here!" Lorena said, ripping some pages out of her book.

"That was your math textbook," Miss Agatha said, no longer smiling. "Very bad, Lorena. Stop that at once. I'll go and get you some nice stationery so you can write proper letters. The princes are not going to want to read around algebra equations."

Maria noticed Gwen and beamed at her. "Hi, Gwennie! I didn't see you come down. Are you going to write letters with us?"

"I'm not sure what I would even say," Gwen admitted. "I also have to leave for my extracurricular study soon."

Jamie rushed to her side. "I can help! Before we ended up going for that gross unplanned swim, I got to learn some stuff about Frederick on our boat ride. If you can stick around for a second, I'll tell you everything I found out!"

"Oh!" Gwen said. She still felt shy about the idea of writing to Frederick, but that was silly. If they were going to be friends, then it made sense to get to know each other. And writing letters was actually a great way to have conversations with no pressure, since they could take their time responding and there wouldn't be any risk of accidental napping or nuzzling. "That would be great, Jamie. Thank you."

By the time she was walking along the now-familiar path in the haunted forest, Gwen was actually excited about the letter idea. Jamie had told her that Frederick liked books and model ships, which was both interesting and surprising. Frederick hadn't said anything about liking to read when the topic came up that first night. But she kept forgetting that he was more introverted than his brothers. And model ships sounded fascinating! She supposed someone needed a lot of attention to detail and dedication to enjoy something like that.

When she arrived at club headquarters, she found the other princesses gathered in the courtyard. Jolie was the first to spot her. (Gwen still wasn't sure how Jolie was able to see at all without actual eyeballs, but she supposed magical curses just had their own special logic.)

"Gwen! Welcome back! How did things go with Frederick?"

"Yes! We want to hear everything!" Syrah added.

Gwen smiled, touched that the other girls had remembered. "Oh, it went perfectly! Thank you all so much again for your help."

Prez walked toward her across the grass. "Hey, great to see you, Gwen. Today's going to be a fun day. We're gonna—"

Abbi ran over and interrupted, "Make potions to reverse our curses!"

That clearly had not been what Prez had been going to say. "What? Abbi, no, we're not doing that."

"Please, Prez! I really, really need to try this today, just this once."

"Is today a special day?" Gwen asked.

Abbi nodded. "Tonight's my school prom. It's basically the most important night in every teenager's life. And when I think about walking onto that dance floor in this stupid cursed body . . . well, I just won't do it. I can't." Gwen's heart twinged for her new friend. It must be so hard to look like an old woman when you were only fifteen.

Then Abbi held up a magazine, pointing to a DIY article she'd opened it to. "But then I found this! It's a recipe for a twenty-four-hour curse-reversal potion! If we make it now, I could have the magical prom night I've always dreamed of."

Prez put a hand on Abbi's shoulder. "Abbi, you know that's

not going to work, right? That article is just preying on people's insecurities to sell magazines! Besides, it completely goes against the ethos of the Cursed Princess Club, which is to love ourselves in our current form."

Abbi shook off Prez's hand, rejecting her words. Gwen had to admit that statement was hard to accept coming from Prez, whose current form was that of a very attractive young woman. Gwen still didn't know what Prez's curse was, but it obviously wasn't something that affected her appearance.

"Yes, fine, in general, we should accept what we look like," Abbi said to the others who had gathered around. "But what if we all got twenty-four hours to be our old selves again? Wouldn't that be amazing, guys?"

There was a lot of excited chatter from the princesses. Prez frowned worriedly.

Thermidora clicked her pincers excitedly. "I could go on a date with my Benedict!"

"I could lie all I want without consequence!" Syrah said, one finger touching her nose, which was just a little longer than normal today.

"Uh, no," Monika said, "your lies would still have consequences. But I could finally order at a fast-food restaurant without turning into a bird!"

Syrah looked at her quizzically. "Ordering fast food makes you that anxious?"

Monika pressed her hands into her cheeks. "They ask so many questions, and everyone in line is waiting impatiently behind me, and . . ."

Prez was still trying to stop this speeding train in its tracks. "But guys—what would Princess Panda say?"

Was she just trying to protect the others from disappointment if the potion didn't work? Or did she have another reason for wanting to prevent this plan? "Prez," Gwen asked, "what would you do if you had your curse removed for twenty-four hours?"

Prez looked away, her face unreadable. "Nothing. I can't take back the things I've done. I can only take my past experiences and try to use them to help others in the present."

Gwen immediately felt terrible for prying. Whatever Prez's curse was, even if it wasn't visible, it clearly upset her. But before she could apologize, Abbi pushed past her and threw her arms around Prez, weeping into her chest.

"Please, Prez! I really, really need this. Just please let us try? I'll never ask for anything again. I promise! All I want is for Bobby to tell me that I'm beautiful and take my hand to dance. Just—just once." She dissolved into sobs.

Prez sighed and patted Abbi's aquamarine hair. "Oh, all right," she said. "But I'm not taking any part in it, okay?"

"Really?" Abbi's sobs dried up at once. "Oh my god, thank you! Thank you, Prez!" She turned to Gwen and grabbed her arm. "Come on, Gwen! We gotta go to the market!"

Gwen let herself be dragged into the trees. She glanced back to see Prez still standing there, staring off at nothing. If Abbi had noticed Prez's uneasiness, she didn't give any sign. She was skipping along excitedly, all traces of her earlier sadness gone. It made sense, though—if this potion really worked, Abbi would be able to have the romantic prom night she'd always dreamed of. It might be her one and only chance.

"Thank you so much for coming with me, Gwen. You like to cook and stuff, so I figured you'd be perfect for helping me pick out the potion ingredients." She handed Gwen the recipe to look at while they walked.

Gwen laughed a little nervously. "Well, I've never cooked with chimera blood or centaur hair, but I'm happy to help!"

It didn't take them long to reach the market. Since Gwen had never been there before—she'd never been brave enough to sneak out with Maria to go shopping—she couldn't help staring around as they walked through the golden gates under the sign that said WELCOME TO PASTEL PLAZA. They stepped onto a wide, central brick road lined with colorful shops on either side. The shops seemed to have almost everything someone could ever need. Books, clothing, all different kinds of food and supplies—she couldn't even take it all in at once. Strangers brushed quickly by on either side of them, focused on their own errands. Gwen stayed close to Abbi as the younger girl pulled her into one store and then another.

After the apothecary, Abbi consulted the list one more time.

"Okay, looks like the last thing we need to get is brandy. Who's Brandy? And what part of her do we cut off and stick in the potion?"

Gwen couldn't quite tell if Abbi was joking. She hoped so. "But that's alcohol! We can't buy that—we're minors!"

Abbi laughed. "Girl, please. Look who you're talking to! No one would even believe me if I said I was fifteen!"

But Gwen was too used to following the rules. This felt wrong. "Abbi, I don't think—"

Abbi's good humor evaporated. "Oh, come on, Gwen! It's not like I want to get drunk or anything! I'm just going to use the alcohol to get a boy from school to make out with me!"

A middle-aged woman walking by with her young son turned to look at Abbi in shock. "No, um, it's okay," Abbi tried to tell her. "I'm younger than I look."

The woman pulled her son quickly away down the road.

"See?" Abbi asked Gwen. "So just wait here, and I'll be right back, okay?" Before Gwen could respond, Abbi marched into the liquor store. She gave a little wave to the man who worked there. "Hey, little boy. Grandma wants to get lit."

Gwen felt super uncomfortable about letting Abbi buy alcohol, but she also understood how important this potion was to her. And Abbi was right; it wasn't like she wanted the brandy to get drunk. It was just one more ingredient in the potion. Still, Gwen felt complicit standing outside the store and waiting there. And she certainly didn't want anyone to think Abbi was buying the alcohol for her! Maybe she should go into one of the other stores while she was waiting. She looked around. There—a cute little shop across the street had some interesting things in the window. Some old books, and an abacus, and—oh! Was that a model ship? Maybe she could find a little something to send to Frederick along with her letter.

A little bell rang as she pushed open the door. "Welcome," said the lady behind the counter. Gwen smiled at her politely and started to peruse the shelves. She'd been in enough stores with Abbi by this point that she knew what to do. She would look around, see what she wanted to buy, and then bring it up to the counter to pay for it. Luckily she always carried a few gems around with her for emergencies, even though she'd never had a reason to use them until now.

There were some really beautiful model ships, but she didn't have enough gems to buy something very expensive, and a large gift would be more difficult to mail. Besides, she didn't want to send the wrong message. A big gift might imply more than she intended. A small token was best.

After some poking around, she found a book she thought Frederick might like and a tiny model ship in a narrow glass bottle. *These are perfect!* she thought happily. The little gifts would hopefully be in line with his interests but also small enough not to make him feel awkward. She brought them to the counter, handed over the gems, and waited while the lady packed her items into a little bag with some tissue paper. By the time she was done, Abbi was waiting for her outside.

Abbi held up a brown paper bag. "I got the goods! Let's head back and make some potion!" She noticed Gwen's own bag. "Oh! Did you buy something from that store?"

"Yes! I found the perfect things to send to Frederick with my letter." She held the bag open for Abbi to peek in.

"A book and a ship in a bottle? This is what Frederick likes?" She shook her head scornfully. "What an old geezer!"

Once again, Gwen couldn't quite tell if Abbi was joking. It didn't matter anyway. Gwen felt confident that Frederick would like her gifts. It wasn't necessary for Abbi or anyone else to understand. Maybe Frederick was a little different from other boys—it wasn't like Gwen had anyone to compare him to except his brothers and her own—but if that was the case, she didn't mind at all.

# CHAPTER 20

## GWENDOLYN

Abbi had shooed everyone else out of the kitchen while she worked on the potion. "No distractions!" she told them as she hurried them out. "One tiny mistake could mess up everything!" Only Gwen had been invited to stay, drafted as Abbi's assistant. Abbi wanted to do all the mixing and measuring herself, but she asked Gwen to read out the instructions as they went along. The counters were covered in used spoons and bowls and splashes of various substances, and they must have used every pot and pan the club owned. Plus the big cauldron, too, of course. Gwen tended to be a tidy cook, cleaning up as she went along, but Abbi had a different approach. Poor Curtis was going to have a fit. They should really offer to help clean up, after.

They'd just boiled the chimera blood with three raccoon molars, and now it had to simmer for five minutes. Abbi set the kitchen timer, which was shaped like a tiny panda head. She was bouncing on her toes, unable to hide her excitement. She leaned close to the stove and whispered to the simmering red liquid. "I'm counting on you, chimera blood!"

Gwen really hoped the potion worked. Abbi deserved her magical night with Bobby. Of all the curses Gwen had learned about so far, Abbi's seemed one of the crueler ones. Who had even given her that sinister box?! There was nothing wrong with being an old woman, of course, but that should come after a long life as a younger person. No fifteen-year-old wanted to look elderly before her time. Looking like an old woman seemed even worse than . . . well, than a lot of things. Abbi's peers wouldn't even see her as one of them anymore. The Cursed Princess Club was probably the only place she could feel truly accepted for who she was.

Prez wanted all of them to accept themselves, too, but somehow that seemed harder. Gwen had no trouble accepting Abbi, but when she thought about herself, about what Frederick had said—

Nope. She wasn't going to think about that. Not now, not ever again. It didn't matter anyway. Frederick didn't have to think she was beautiful if they were just going to be friends. He could think whatever he wanted. Even that she was—

The panda timer went off, and Abbi grabbed the handle of the pot with a polygon-patterned potholder. She dumped the hot blood and teeth carefully into the cauldron. Gwen peered into the potion in progress, which was currently a muddy brown color. It did *not* smell good. The aroma had gotten worse with each new ingredient, so she didn't anticipate any improvements at this point. But then she supposed whoever wrote potion recipes was understandably focused on magical results, not smell or taste.

"Okay," Abbi said. "What's next?"

Gwen consulted the magazine. "Adding in the newt eyeballs."

"Newt eyeballs . . ." Abbi muttered, looking around. "Where did we put those again?"

"If the vial's not here, it should be in the bag on the coffee table," Gwen said.

Abbi darted into the living room and returned a moment later. "Got it!" She emptied the vial's contents into the cauldron. "And now?"

"Count slowly to twenty-four while staring intently into the potion," Gwen said, checking the recipe again. "And then the last thing is sprinkling in the chopped phoenix feathers." She set down the magazine on one of the few relatively unsplattered surfaces she could find.

Abbi locked her eyes on the bubbling liquid. "One . . . two . . . three . . ."

Gwen made sure the chopped feathers were close at hand while Abbi finished counting. The other girl's surging anticipation was contagious. Gwen found herself eagerly imagining how happy everyone would be to set their curses aside, even if only for one day.

"Twenty-four!" Abbi finished, a little breathlessly. She grabbed the chopped feathers and sprinkled them in. There was an immediate poof of smoke, and the potion turned a vibrant purple color.

"Okay!" Abbi said. "I think it's done!" She was practically radiating hope and faith. "Hey, everyone!" she called. "Who wants to try a twenty-four-hour curse-reversal potion?"

There was a chorus of eager voices calling "Me!" from the living room.

Abbi began ladling single servings of the potion into heat-resistant glasses.

"Hey, Prez," Saffron called, noticing their president heading for the door, "don't you want to get in on this?"

Prez didn't stop walking. "No, thanks. I'm going to go chop some firewood. You guys have fun, though!"

The others all gathered around the kitchen island.

"Okay," Abbi said. "Everyone who wants to participate should take a piece of paper"—she indicated a stack of pre-cut notebook paper she and Gwen had prepared earlier—"and write down a specific wish or reason they want their curse reversed. After that, each person must drink a full cup of potion and kiss their scrap of paper. The potion will take effect shortly after the kiss and will last for exactly twenty-four hours. And Gwen'll be watching over us just in case anything goes awry. Because she's the best."

Gwen felt her face go warm, but it was a nice kind of warm. "It's the least I can do after everything you guys helped me with," she said.

Abbi picked up one of the potion servings and raised it to the room. "So everyone take a glass, and let's do this!"

Everyone cheered and whooped and crowded around to grab glasses and pieces of paper. Then they all spread out to write down their reasons.

"I want to try on mascara," Jolie said.

"I want to be able to walk outside without making obscene hand gestures to people on the street," Saffron said.

Abbi had already scrawled her reason on her paper. "There's only one thing I've ever wanted," she said, her expression full of longing. "I want to walk into my school auditorium in my uncursed teenage body and a glittery dress, and have Bobby come over to me and say, 'Abbi, I think you're beautiful. Will you dance with me?'"

Then she tossed back her shot of potion, made a face at the taste, picked up her paper, and kissed it really hard. For a very long time.

"Abbi," Gwen whispered finally, "you've been kissing that paper for like five minutes. I think you're good."

The others had finished their writing and drinking by that point. There had been a number of groans and grimaces at the grossness of the potion, but no one complained. They all looked full of hope and anticipation. Gwen realized that even though the group usually seemed pretty upbeat in general, they were probably always struggling at least a little bit to make peace with their curses. It couldn't be easy to go through life with a goblin hand, or without eyes, or never knowing when your anxiety was going to turn you into a crow against your will.

They all sat back and waited.

"I'm so excited!" Syrah said.

"It should be any second now," Abbi assured her.

But the seconds kept ticking by, and nothing happened. After a while, people began drifting off, finding things to do to pass the time. Saffron went downstairs to practice his Ping-Pong serve. Syrah closed her eyes and took a nap. Only Abbi stayed where she was, eyes open, unmoving.

Monika had gone to the kitchen table with the leftover paper scraps. Now she came over to Gwen, holding up some really impressive paper flowers linked into a chain. "I made you a paper necklace," she said shyly.

"Wow, Monika!" Gwen looped it around her neck gratefully.

"Yeah, I wrote down that if I didn't turn into a crow from anxiety, my wish would be to someday open a jewelry store. Here, take a look!" She handed Gwen a small, pink hand mirror.

Gwen took the mirror and gasped. She barely heard Monika asking, "Do you like it?"

"Oh my god, *no*," Gwen whispered.

Her reflection was broken in this mirror too. Instead of her own familiar eyes, all she saw was shattered emptiness. She tried changing the angle of the mirror and shifting her position, but nothing made a difference. She could see the edge of her mouth, her ears . . . but everything else was a horrible black nothing with jagged lines like broken glass stretching out in all directions. Like the mirror couldn't bear to contain her reflection. Or maybe like she wasn't really there at all. Like she didn't even exist.

She touched its surface, like she had with the mirror at home, but it felt smooth and solid and completely normal. She tilted it, trying to capture some of the others, and it reflected them just fine.

Which meant there wasn't just something wrong with her bedroom mirror. There was something wrong with her.

She was pulled out of her spiraling thoughts by Thermidora's resonant voice. "Um, Abbi, darling? While that was quite a delicious hair-and-teeth tea, wasn't the purpose to make our curses vanish? Why am I still in this repulsive, voluptuous human flesh? And why has Monika turned into a bird again?"

Gwen looked at Monika, startled. When had she turned into a crow? Hadn't they just been talking—?

Abbi finally seemed to have lost any remaining shreds of hope. "Sorry, everyone. I—I didn't mean to waste your time." She was talking to the floor, her eyes blinking back tears. "I guess this means I'm not going to my prom after all."

Gwen sat down beside her. "Are you sure you don't still want to go? Even just to see your classmates?"

"No. I'll just kill the mood if I go looking like this. I think I'm just gonna go up to bed now."

Jolie hurried over. "Um, actually, before you go upstairs, Prez said she'd like to speak to you outside."

Abbi sighed. "Great. Now I get to have a lecture about why I shouldn't have been tricked by a stupid magazine. Isn't being stuck in this body punishment enough?" But she headed obediently in the direction Jolie had pointed.

"Abbi . . ." Gwen began, but she didn't really know how to finish. She felt so bad for the other girl. She watched Abbi open the garden door.

"Listen, Prez," Abbi said, "I get it, I—" Then she stopped and just stood there, staring.

Gwen craned her neck to see what Abbi was looking at. Prez was standing in the doorway, and behind her, the garden had been transformed. Small cocktail tables wrapped in purple fabric had been set up with vases of flowers and elegant candelabras. Strings of glowing lights and streamers decorated the trees and draped from the eaves of the house, and purple and white balloons were scattered everywhere. The effect was incredible. It was like they'd all been transported to another place, one explicitly designed for dancing and laughing and having fun.

"I'm no Bobby," Prez said, "but I think you're beautiful just the way you are, Abbi." She reached out a hand. "Will you dance with me?"

Gwen could see just enough of Abbi's face from her angle to watch an enormous smile spread across it. "Yes," she whispered.

Prez smiled back. "Curtis, if you would?"

Curtis appeared from around the side of the house holding a violin. "Right away, Your Highness."

Curtis was apparently a talented musician as well as a chef and everything else, because the music he played was heavenly. Prez and Abbi began to dance. Prez was smiling, and Abbi was laughing through her tears. Gwen didn't know what Abbi had looked like before her curse, but she really did look beautiful right then.

"Shall we join them, girls?" Syrah asked.

Jolie nodded eagerly. "Looks like we're having a dance party!"

Everyone ran toward the patio. Gwen hesitated, but Jolie grabbed her hand and pulled her forward. "Come on, Gwen! You don't want to sit this one out!"

And then suddenly Gwen was dancing in a circle with the other princesses, holding hands with Jolie and Monika, laughing at Syrah's over-the-top gyrations and at Saffron's unwilling participation in Thermidora's demonstration of the lobster courtship dance, feeling a kind of joy she hadn't felt in . . . well, maybe ever.

She had always had her family, but she had never had *this*—this community and companionship and mutual support of a group of people who chose to be together not because of blood ties but because they wanted to. She had never had *friends*. These girls—and Saffron—accepted her because they liked her, because they thought she had value as a person, because they felt she was worth having around. They didn't care where she came from or what she looked like or even what she could do or not do. They liked who she was on the inside, and they believed that was really all that mattered. She wondered if she could someday believe that too.

She was twirling around with the others, drinking in the music and the night, when she suddenly spied Nell from the corner of her eye. The Striped princess wasn't dancing; she only glared at them from the shadows. It almost seemed like she was glaring at Gwen specifically, but that didn't make any sense. She didn't even know Gwen! Jolie had said that Nell tended to do her own thing; she must just not like big groups. Maybe she was upset by the noise of the music like she had been by the slumber party. But if so, she didn't say anything. Maybe even Nell could see how important this night was to Abbi.

When Gwen next turned around, Nell was gone. Gwen decided not to waste any more time thinking about her. She just wanted to focus on the music and her new friends and all the good feelings that were welling up inside her. Her path to the Cursed Princess Club may have been a rocky one, and some parts were still too painful to dwell on, but it had all been worth it to get her to this moment. Gwen closed her eyes and spun to the music, laughing with her friends, having the best night of her life.

# CHAPTER 21

## FREDERICK

Father was screaming at him. Again.

"This? This is your proposal for the future growth of our kingdom's prosperity? This atrocity?!" He crumpled the papers in his fist and his voice dropped to a cold calmness. "I take back all those words of pride and acknowledgment I had for you recently, Frederick."

Frederick stared at the carpet, knowing better than to meet his father's eyes when he was this angry. He didn't understand what he'd done wrong, but that was nothing new. He thought his plan for more trees and libraries was a great way to look toward the Plaid Kingdom's future. What could be more beneficial than natural spaces and books and education? The libraries could even become community centers, hosting events and—

But Father was yelling again. "Lance has been handing in manlier proposals since before he learned to tie his own shoes!"

Ah, so that was it. Father wanted something involving war or soldiers or building giant defensive walls.

The king thrust the crumped papers into Frederick's chest. "There is a great deal you could stand to learn from your brothers. You'll be shadowing them today during their daily duties. And I can only pray that a sliver of their excellence will seep into that malnourished little body of yours."

The crumpled papers fluttered to the floor. They both watched them for a moment. Then the king said, "Pick up your mess too." With that he turned and strode away.

Frederick knelt and gathered the pages of his proposal. He supposed he should have known Father wouldn't be interested in trees and libraries. It had seemed like such a good idea, though! For once he'd actually gotten excited about this annual proposal assignment, and that excitement had only grown as he was researching and writing up his plans. He could envision all the new green in the landscape, the beautiful open spaces, the stately libraries filled with every kind of book people in the kingdom could possibly want.

He shook his head, feeling stupid. As usual. He was never going to please his father with ideas like that. But then, he was probably never going to please his father anyway. He was never going to be enough like his brothers. And his father wasn't interested in what else Frederick might have to offer. He only cared that Frederick was smaller and weaker and not good at any of the right things.

Frederick knew he should be grateful for his lot in life. He knew most people thought it would be amazing to be royalty, that if he was a prince then certainly he must feel blessed. But if literally all the people you've ever been allowed to associate with and are constantly compared to are also royalty and are better in every way than you are . . . well, what his life actually felt like was a curse.

Later that morning he reported to the blue ballroom to assist Blaine with whatever important princely thing was on the agenda. He pulled open the heavy golden door and stepped inside to find his brother posing on a dais, dressed like a merman.

Frederick stopped and stared.

Blaine was naked from the waist up except for a red plaid bow tie around his neck. From the waist down his body was encased in a very convincing fish-tail costume. He held a trident in one hand and was making a manly fist with the other, all the while smiling handsomely at the portrait artist who was practically in tears at the beautiful specimen he was fortunate enough to get to paint. There was an ocean-colored curtain behind him that had the word *MERMAY* displayed in sexy green uppercase letters. At the far end of the ballroom, behind a velvet rope, a crowd of young women watched and panted and drooled. The ones in front held a huge sign that said THE OFFICIAL PRINCE BLAINE FAN CLUB.

"*This* is your important royal duty?" Frederick asked when he could finally speak again.

"Oh, I'm sorry," Blaine said through his flawless smile, "does *your* personal brand bring in two percent of the national GDP and raise awareness for multiple charitable foundations? Hmm? This is for my annual fundraising calendar."

Frederick deflated, his outrage draining out of him to be immediately replaced with his usual feelings of idiocy and inadequacy.

"No," he admitted. "But—what do you even need help with?"

The painter handed him some fake seaweed props with fake little clown fish swimming around on them. "Hold these up in the background." He told Frederick where to stand and then directed him to crouch awkwardly until the seaweed was in the perfect position. Or at least as close to perfect as it was likely to get. The painter never seemed completely happy with Frederick's seaweed portrayal, even though he really was trying to follow the directions exactly.

In the afternoon, he went to assist Lance with his sparring session. He didn't quite understand why sparring was an important princely duty either. At least Blaine had been raising funds for good causes. Lance was just working out. Like he did all the time.

Frederick's muscles began shaking after only a few minutes of holding up the pads for Lance to punch and kick. It didn't help that his arms were already tired from carrying those stupid seaweed props for so long. But even at his best, he was nowhere near as strong as Lance, of course. And that was fine, or at least, it should have been. There had been a time when he'd simply looked up to his brothers. When he'd admired Blaine's perfection and Lance's strength and hadn't felt like such a loser in comparison. He supposed that was a long time ago now, though. When had he started feeling this way?

"It's cool you're helping me out, li'l bro, but you kind of look like you're dying right now." Lance shook his head. "How were you able to survive your military academy training?"

"I'm fine!" Frederick said without thinking. "I don't need you to go easy on me!" This was, of course, a lie, but he couldn't seem to back down, even when Lance was clearly offering him a way out. "And I specialized in administrative support!"

"Oh, I see," Lance said, smiling wolfishly. "Well, then, thanks for supporting me as I administrate this *kick*!" He punctuated that last word with action, his foot whipping out so fast that Frederick had no time to prepare. He went flying, and then his head smacked painfully against something hard and then everything got very weird and dark.

"Oh my god! I'm sorry, Frederick! Are you all right?" He could hear Lance speaking, but it was faint in the darkness. And it seemed like far too much effort to try to respond. It was nice that Lance cared, though. His concern actually seemed genuine.

Frederick's mind drifted, and he found himself thinking back to that earlier question of when, exactly, he had started feeling like a loser. But he knew the answer to that, didn't he? The memory was never far from his mind.

It had been his very first day of military academy. Blaine and Lance had already been attending for years, racking up medals and accolades, but Frederick had been homeschooled all of that time due to his famously weak constitution. He was alone for a lot of his childhood, but other than missing his brothers, he hadn't minded all that much. He'd spent that time enveloped in the vivid worlds of his books, and he loved it.

When he was twelve, his father finally decided he was healthy enough to go to school, although for some reason not the same school as Blaine and Lance. He enrolled Frederick mid-semester at St. Cerulean's Inter-Kingdom Military Academy for Royal Boys.

Frederick had been so excited. He felt shame wash over him as he remembered how naive he'd been. That first day, he'd been invited to stand at the front of the class to introduce himself. He'd gushed about his favorite books and even held up a copy of *The Little Prawnce*, his favorite of all time. It had never occurred to him that his enthusiasm wouldn't be well received and reciprocated by his classmates.

He'd felt so happy, walking back to his room. He'd already unpacked and set everything up, so he was looking forward to relaxing and reading for the rest of the night. But when he got there, he found some of the other boys waiting for him. Even then, he hadn't realized what was about to happen.

"Hey, Sunflower," one of them said, roughly tousling Frederick's unruly yellow hair as if to emphasize what inspired the new nickname. "We just wanted to give you a warm welcome to our school. Nice room you have here. Think you got enough books?"

"Thanks," Frederick said, so pleased to be making new friends already. "I was actually thinking I should have brought more—"

"Shut up!" the boy said, shoving him toward his companions, who laughed meanly. "I was making fun of you!"

The other boys began shoving him too. "Ugh," one of them said, "there's nothing worse than a dork who doesn't know he is one!"

The first boy shoved him again, and this time he fell backward into his open trunk. "So hey, Sunflower," the boy said, staring down at Frederick, who was finally beginning to feel afraid, "since you read so much, tell me . . . do you know how long it takes for a sunflower to wilt in the dark?"

Frederick looked up at their faces, took in their cruel expressions, tried to understand what was happening. "Um, I don't really read botanical books, so—"

And then the lid of the trunk slammed down, trapping him in darkness.

"It just takes one night," he heard the lead boy say.

"Let me out!" Frederick cried. He could hear sounds—awful, confusing sounds of smashing and tearing—but one of them must have been holding the trunk closed, because he couldn't push the lid open. "What are you doing out there? Let me out, please!"

Eventually he stopped pounding on the inside of the trunk, stopped begging, stopped everything. He just waited. And once it finally grew quiet, he cautiously tried the lid once more. This time it opened without resistance. He climbed out into his ruined room, staring sadly at his destroyed belongings . . . especially the books, every one of which had been ripped to shreds.

*They were right*, he thought now in the weird darkness, which was very similar to the darkness of being locked inside the trunk. It had only taken one night for him to wilt.

That night had established his role as a loser, both for himself and for everyone else. None of the other boys would talk to him or even acknowledge his existence. He'd tried writing to Father for advice, but all he got back was a single page that said SINK OR SWIM, SON in disturbing uppercase letters that looked like they'd been written in blood.

So he'd decided to sink. He got more books and a better lock for his door. He dreamed of sailing away on one of his model ships and pretended he was the protagonist in every book he bought or borrowed from the library. And he became obsessed with one particular fairy tale about a man who lived at the bottom of a deep hole in the ground. The man couldn't climb out no matter how much he tried, and for that he was the laughingstock of the village. Frederick hadn't even had to pretend to be that protagonist. The story summed up exactly how he felt about himself and his life.

But then one day, an angel of fortune as beautiful and radiant as a thousand suns appeared above the man, and she reached down and lifted him out. With her by his side, the man became admired and respected by everyone. With her faith in him, the man gained courage he never knew he had and defeated a giant serpent that had been terrorizing the village. He was crowned a hero and lived happily ever after with the angel of fortune forever by his side.

Frederick had read that story so many times, trying to make himself believe that someday someone would come to save him too. But as the years went on, he realized he was an idiot to believe in such stupid things. He made it through school, but without any honors or accolades, much to his father's exasperation. He continued to sink in comparison to his brothers in terms of achievement, popularity, and self-worth. He knew he was responsible for all of it. He was choosing to remain in his hole. But why should he keep trying to impress people who never supported him? If everyone was going to look down on him anyway, then he would just beat them to it. He would look down on everything and everyone first. Including himself. Forever. Why not?

But then Father had shown them the portrait of the princesses from the Pastel Kingdom. He'd seen Jamie's image, and he'd immediately thought she—he—was the angel of fortune he'd dreamed would come for him. Frederick had thought he'd lost hope, but apparently a tiny spark of it remained, buried deep within, and now it flared to life. With this angel by his side, he would be just like the man in the story—he'd become admired and respected and finally grow into the man he knew he could be.

But then of course it had all gone wrong. When he'd learned the truth about who he was actually supposed to marry, he realized he'd vastly underestimated how cruel fate could be. Gwendolyn hadn't come to save him. At worst, she was a witch from a different type of fairy tale who had come to bring him a life of horror and despair. And even if she wasn't really a witch, her physical appearance wouldn't bring him admiration but would instead just drag him deeper into the hole as the village loser. He could almost feel it happening already, her clawed fingers grasping his ankles and pulling him backward into the depths as he scrambled desperately, trying to get away. The image was so real that he screamed—

—and found himself sitting up in bed, his brothers looking down at him.

"Oh, you're awake!" Blaine said. He thrust a glass of water toward Frederick's face. "Here, drink some fluids."

"Wait," Frederick said. He was so disoriented and exhausted, but his heart was still pounding from the . . . dream? Had it been a dream? "What happened? Why are we in my room?"

"You passed out when you were sparring with Lance," Blaine said.

"And we felt bad for pushing you so hard when you were assisting us," Lance added. "But also, we came to give you this!" He handed Frederick a parcel wrapped in brown paper and tied with a green ribbon. "Check it out, we each got packages in the mail from the Pastel princesses!"

"Yours was the heaviest, by the way," Blaine said.

"Yeah," Lance said, "heavy like you and Gwen were about to get on that couch—"

"*Shut it, Lance!* I told you that's not what was happening!"

Lance held up his hands in surrender, backing toward the door. "All right, all right, sorry. We'll leave you to read your love letter in peace."

"Take it easy, Frederick," Blaine said. "Good work, today."

They left and closed the door behind them.

"Thanks," Frederick said softly. Blaine had actually sounded sincere. And Lance—well, Lance loved to get under his skin, but he also knew that Lance wouldn't bother if he didn't actually care about him. His brothers weren't so bad, really.

He looked down at the package in his lap. The package from Gwendolyn. Who was turning out to be even more confounding than he'd imagined. At their last visit to the Pastel Palace, she had been the most horrifying part. But also, somehow, the only nice part. She was incredibly thoughtful and kind. Not to mention ridiculously good at making soup. Had he somehow gotten the wrong impression of her? Blaine did always get annoyed at him for his overactive imagination.

But even so, being kind didn't really count much for anything in this world. *Sorry, Gwendolyn,* he thought, pulling the green ribbon and starting to unwrap the package. *Even if we are arranged to be together, I can't give you anything you need. And there's simply nothing of real value that you could—*

He gasped.

The paper had fallen away to reveal a book. And not just any book. *The Little Prawnce.* His favorite from childhood. He'd never gotten another copy after his classmates destroyed the first one. How could she have known? But there was a letter too. He picked it up and started to read.

*Hi, Frederick. I heard you enjoy reading, so I thought I would send one of my favorite books. I'm afraid it may be too childish for your tastes, but it's a story that always makes me feel nice. What are your favorite books? I also included a small charm at the bottom of the bag. I hope you like it! Warm regards, Gwen.*

He stared at the book, tracing the shape of the prawn on the cover with his finger. She wanted to know about his favorite books. He'd never shared that with anyone again after that day at school. But if she liked this book as much as he did, maybe it couldn't hurt to tell her just a few other good ones. Titles were already scrolling through his mind, begging to be written down and sent to her.

He realized he was smiling and couldn't remember the last time that had happened. He felt—he didn't know how to describe it. Despite everything that had happened, all his disappointment and unhappiness, somehow Gwendolyn could make him feel . . . what was the word he was searching for?

He reached into the bottom of the bag she'd sent, feeling around for the charm she'd mentioned. His fingers closed around what felt like a small glass tube. He pulled it out, and his breath caught in his chest.

It was full of eyeballs. Tiny, round, white eyeballs, each with a tiny black pupil in the center.

*Terrified*, he decided. That was the name of the feeling. Gwendolyn made him feel terrified.

He sat there in his bed, trembling, for a very long time.

# EPILOGUE

Later that night, at the CPC headquarters, Abbi and Monika sat at the dining room table. The princess prom had been amazing, and some of the others were still dancing even now, but Abbi needed a breather. She tried to ignore the old-ladyness of her body as much as possible, but sometimes it got inside her head and made her feel like she didn't have the energy of a normal fifteen-year-old.

Monika made a weird sound beside her.

"You okay?" Abbi asked. She was never sure with Monika what was a bird thing and what was a girl thing.

"Yeah," Monika said. "I think so. My stomach feels a little wonky. Probably from drinking that icky potion." Her stomach voiced its agreement, gurgling loudly. They both giggled.

Then Monika suddenly made a lemon-sucking face and spit something out of her mouth. It landed on the table.

"Gross," Abbi said conversationally.

Monika looked mortified. "What is that?"

It was a tiny toy ship. Abbi stared at it, feeling a nagging sense of familiarity. She had seen that ship somewhere before. Where—?

And then she knew. It was the dumb little ship in a bottle that Gwen had bought for that jerky prince. She had purchased it on their shopping trip to get ingredients for the potion. It had been in a bag on the coffee table. The same coffee table where they'd left some of the other bags from that afternoon. And now that she thought of it, the bottle the ship had been in had really been more like a vial. Kind of the same exact size and shape of the vial of newt eyeballs, in fact.

No wonder the curse-reversal potion hadn't worked. She must have reached into Gwen's bag by accident, grabbed the ship vial thinking it was the eyeballs, and then dumped it into the cauldron without realizing. Which meant maybe the potion *would* have worked! Although Prez still seemed pretty sure that there was no such thing as a real twenty-four-hour curse-reversal potion. Abbi decided to believe that, because otherwise she'd have to believe that she'd ruined her own magical night by messing up the ingredients, and she really couldn't face that idea right now.

But if she'd put Gwen's toy ship into the potion, what had Gwen sent to her reluctant fiancé?

*Oh . . . oh no.*

# ABOUT THE AUTHOR

Michelle Knudsen is the *New York Times* best-selling author of more than fifty books for children and young adults, including the award-winning picture book *Library Lion*, which was selected by *Time* magazine as one of the 100 Best Children's Books of All Time. Her novels include *The Dragon of Trelian* (VOYA Top Shelf Fiction for Middle School Readers) and *Evil Librarian* (YALSA Best Fiction for Young Adults; Sid Fleischman Award for Humor). Michelle also sometimes writes short fiction for adults and was a 2024 BSFA (British Science Fiction Association) finalist for the audio version of her short story "The Pigeon." Her most recent title is the picture book *Luigi, the Spider Who Wanted to Be a Kitten*, illustrated by Kevin Hawkes, and her next book will be the middle grade fantasy novel, *Into the Wild Magic* (Candlewick Press, August 2025). Michelle teaches writing in Lesley University's low-residency MFA program. She lives in Brooklyn, New York, with three humans, two cats, and one snake.